BARBARA:
Sarah's Legacy

by James D. Yoder

BERLIN MENNONITE CHURCH
96028

Newton, Kansas

Other Faith & Life Press books
by James D. Yoder

The Yoder Outsiders
Sarah of the Border Wars

Barbara: Sarah's Legacy

Copyright © 1994 by Faith & Life Press, Newton, Kansas 67114-0347. This publication may not be reproduced, stored in a retrieval system, or transmitted in whole or in part, in any form by any means, electronic, mechanical, photocopying, recording, or otherwise without prior permission of Faith & Life Press.

Printed in the United States of America

97 96 95 94 4 3 2 1

Library of Congress Number 93-74685

International Standard Book Number 0-87303-214-4

This is a work of fiction built around historical events; any similarities to persons presently living is coincidental.

Editorial direction for Faith & Life Press by Susan E. Janzen; copyediting by Edna Krueger Dyck; design by John Hiebert; printing by Mennonite Press. Cover art by Joy Dunn Keenan.

DEDICATION

To Lonabelle Christine Jantzi Yoder, who
came from upstate New York to Cass County, Missouri, in
the August heat of 1955, wearing a long-sleeved
nylon dress and a smile on her face.

A Note from the Author

Barbara: Sarah's Legacy continues the story begun in *Sarah of the Border Wars*. The setting for the story and the themes and attitudes expressed in the book were established in the first volume.

This is a work of fiction, yet at the same time, it is historical. I knew Barbara Yoder. She was born during the Civil War days. She did enjoy picking gooseberries in the woods. However, in real life, neither Barbara nor her sister, Salome, ever married. They were known for their famous farmstead with its large house and grand Swiss barn.

Many of the accounts regarding the Mennonite youth who were drafted during World War 1 are delivered accurately. I personally heard accounts by members of the Sycamore Grove Mennonite Church about being harassed, ministers jailed, and the tar and feathering of at least one member during those painful times.

It was also narrated to me that women of the community interceded with the judge for more understanding, and as a result, the Mennonite women made noble efforts to raise $1,500 per month for the Red Cross for the duration of the war.

The trip in Barbara's fabulous car is fictional. But the "teeth episode" actually happened to a Mennonite woman from that community on her trip westward. The "sparrow mites" episode in the first chapter is also based on an event that actually happened.

In addition, though fictionalized, I have patterned Simon, who receives a doctorate in theology and becomes a college president, after the noted Dr. J.E. Hartzler, who came from this Cass County, Missouri, community.

Also, an ordained Mennonite clergywoman presently living on the west coast, Joyce Miller Wyse, is a grandniece of Barbara Yoder. She was born on Barb Yoder's place before her family moved to Idaho in 1937.

I had the joy to move onto Barbara's farm in that year, 1937. Because of my great love for the land, the woods and creeks, the wonderful hickory nuts, walnuts, blackberries, gooseberries, and even pawpaws, it was necessary to, as in *Sarah of the Border Wars,* place this story on that particular farm.

I also have tried to reflect the decades of change in the Mennonite church of that community.

This is a story of ordinary people, who are at times extraordinary. It is a story of Christian faith and of songs in the heart.

James D. Yoder

CREDITS

Chapter 3 The quote, "No longer are there jingoes and pacifists, etc.," is from *The Cass County Democrat,* April 19, 1917.

Chapter 5 Events of the draft, especially dates and background information regarding young Mennonite men and World War 1 are from *War, Peace and Nonresistance* by Guy F. Hershberger (Scottdale, Pa.: Herald Press, 1946), p. 121ff.

Lyrics to the song "Good-Bye Ma!" are by William Herschell in 1917 and set to music by Barclay Walker. Published in *The History of Missouri, Vol. II* by David March (New York: Lewis Historical Publishing Company, 1907), p. 1293.

Background information and details regarding conscripted young Mennonite men at Camp Funston are based on "The Treatment of Conscientious Objectors During World War One—Mennonites at Camp Funston" by Sarah D. Shields, an unpublished manuscript in the Mennonite Library and Archives, North Newton, Kansas.

The hymn "Loving Kindness" by Samuel Medley is from the *Church Hymnal* (Scottdale, Pa.: Mennonite Publishing House, 1927), no. 2.

Chapter 9 The hymn "O Lamb of God, Still Keep Me" by James G. Deck is from the *Church Hymnal* (Scottdale, Pa.: Mennonite Publishing House, 1927), no. 447.

The event regarding the Mennonite girls who looked at dresser sets in the jewelry store is based on an event described in Nellie Yoder Roth's written memoirs.

Chapter 18 The hymn "O Sometimes the Shadows Are Deep" by E. Johnson is from the *Church Hymnal* (Scottdale, Pa.: Mennonite Publishing House, 1927), no. 430.

Chapter 19 The hymn "Still Still with Thee" by Harriet B. Stowe is from the *Church Hymnal* (Scottdale, Pa.: Mennonite Publishing House, 1927), no. 196.

Chapter 1

Barbara Yoder hoped her place looked fit and proper for out-of-state company. Samantha Hertzler from Ohio would soon be rolling in with Barbara's nieces, Twili and Mary Barb.

Barbara hoped one or two of her peacocks would fly up on the barn and spread their gorgeous tails to welcome Samantha. That would make her swell with pride. She'd show that Easterner that some beauty and culture could indeed spread itself west of the Mississippi River.

Though she had passed her fiftieth year, Barbara was still trim. She sat for a moment on the porch swing, as the wind touched her grey hair, done up in the same way all those years—in a bun on the back of her head.

She hadn't intended to sit there long, just a moment to catch her breath after the rush of the early morning hours. But she'd slipped into a daydream and sat suspended there in her swing as her mind wandered . . . . "I can remember when Abraham Lincoln was president," she announced one Sunday to her spellbound nieces and nephews who had come over for dinner.

Truthfully, she didn't recollect the Civil War herself. But she had heard the stories her parents, Solomon and Sarah Yoder, told so many times that pretty soon they became her stories, too. They had told her lots of stories about the border wars between Missouri and Kansas Territory—between the bloodthirsty bushwhackers and the jayhawkers.

Barbara finally cleared her head, braced her heels on the porch boards and rose to get on with the day. She decided that it was time to take her brother Noah's children on an all-day outing over beyond Kohler Hill to Harrisonville, where her sister Nancy, who had died during those Civil War years, lay buried.

She glanced at the green corn glistening in her field. Cattails at the edge of the pond nodded in the wind. Beyond, the hedgerow rose up in brilliant green. Her red, stone barn loomed up, sturdy and prosperous looking. She had gotten along just fine since her sister Salome had married Mose Lehman last year. Thanks to the hired man and her nephew, Simon, her place looked fit and proper, even if she did have to say so herself.

But Barbara was a bit nervous about her company from Ohio. Folks from the eastern states sometimes teased these Missouri Mennonites: "Oh, the mud. How do you live with it?" Or, "My, do you still use that outhouse?" She knew they didn't mean to criticize, but such remarks were enough to give a body a twinge, anyway.

Barbara shifted her shoulders. Why hadn't she gone ahead and put in one of those new flush toilets in her upstairs bathroom? She could certainly afford it. She'd just felt that for her it was too much. A person had to draw the line somewhere. Racing to the privy when the temperature got down to fifteen degrees below zero and hunching herself over one of those holes in the three-holer did keep her humble.

Well, she decided, Samantha would have to take her as she was—and that included the outhouse out there by the plum thicket.

Barbara pondered other changes going on around her. The fast pace made her dizzy. How was a person supposed to keep up with all those automobiles whizzing up and down the roads? A blessing, wasn't it, that the county had never cut that road through by her place over beyond Camp Branch and Clearfork? It had saved her a lot of dust.

The young people had started a Literary Society. That was just fine with her—she believed in reading. And her nephew Simon? That boy was going to amount to something someday. He talked about going to high school and had sent off for a catalog from some theological school at Hartford, Connecticut.

Barbara kept up with her own reading, too. She needed to know what was going on beyond Cass County, Missouri. So she took the *Capper's Weekly,* a marvelous little farm paper. She read all about politics as well as the latest crop and livestock prices. She would like to march up the steps leading to the White House and meet that new president—Woodrow Wilson. Never could she remember a president so interested in the peace of the whole world.

She didn't want it told around, but a while back when Barbara and her nephew Simon drove the buggy over to Harrisonville, they had gone to that brick building with the glass windows and looked at a Model T Ford. Sat in it, too. Simon figured that if Aunt Barb bought it, he'd be her driver. Pshaw. If Barbara spent her hard-earned cash for a new Model T Ford, guess who would be driving it?

If you listened closely, beneath the sighing of the wind, you could hear Ezra Hostetler's new Farmall tractor with lug wheels moaning and bouncing across the fields, ripping the sod open with two plowshares behind it. Barbara thought it was wonderful. She remembered when she and Salome used to lead old Dink while their mother held the worn plow handles and plowed ten acres. She had struggled so behind that plow in the heat.

Change was happening everywhere, even at the church. The menfolk had actually torn down the waist-high wooden partition that separated the women's side of the church from the men's. No longer would she have to fool around trying to unhook that little door at the back if she wanted to say something to the bishop face-to-face. And no sooner had they built that long horse shed back along the fence at the churchyard than folks started driving in with automobiles.

Telephones had come to rural Missouri, too. The wires swooped and drooped up and down on all sorts of trees and poles throughout the neighborhood. Learning how to ring your neighbor was complicated. Some called it "crank and holler." Barbara didn't care. She liked her wall telephone, only she didn't rightly care for the way Effie Hooley down the way sapped the strength from her phone by lifting the receiver whenever Barbara's ring came in. But Barbara forgave her. It was a good way to get the news. Everything has a price, doesn't it?

Having Simon live with her meant more washing. But she had one of those hand-operated washing machines out in the summer kitchen. With this new machine she didn't at all mind doing laundry for her nephew. And she learned how a teenager eats. "Pass the roast beef, Auntie Barb, and more potatoes and gravy." Barbara thought it was wonderful to have someone here who enjoyed her good cooking. Her hired man, Abram Zook, usually just sat there with his elbows on the table and shoveled in his vittles so fast that she couldn't rightly take much pleasure in such eating.

Her nieces, Twili and Mary Barb, came over every Thursday to help her clean the big house. Twili generally churned the butter, too. Barbara had saved a lot of money since she had more butter to sell.

Praise the Lord, these were prosperous times. In her orchard, three kinds of apple trees reached up to the sky. The pear trees, drooping with fruit, swept low. Have to sell some of those pears since I still have pear butter and preserves left from last year, Barbara thought to herself.

Barbara remembered when her brother Noah Yoder was chosen by lot to become a preacher in the church. Talk about a long service. Three men had been selected by the congregation. Somehow, when it came time for casting the lot, Barbara knew that Noah would be chosen.

Noah was a pious man and Nettie was a pious sister-in-law. God made Noah Yoder into a good preacher. One thing was for certain. You could hear Noah when he opened his mouth. He always spoke plainly, with a strong voice. Folks listened and nodded their heads.

And how the singing had improved since they'd been having singing schools at church every fall and singing gatherings at Jacob Schrock's on Saturday nights. The young folks would gather around dining room tables on Sunday afternoons and evenings to sing hymns in full four-part harmony.

Barbara let Simon help her get the notes straight. "Don't give me the book with the shaped notes in it. I'll do it right, like I run my farm," she told Simon. So Barbara and Simon sang their "do, re, mi's" until the old farm woman got it right.

Of course a woman had never led singing in their meetinghouse. They still belonged to the Amish Mennonite conference, but Barbara knew progress was being made. She knew that someday a woman—someone who could make your spine tingle with her voice, like Mary Barb—would be up there in front, beating the time with a lifted arm. She might not be as bold as a man like Homer Wenger, but she would be up there, leading the singing graciously and piously. Barbara believed that verse her mother used to quote about how there is neither male nor female in Christ, but that all are one.

Then there were the wind-powered generators that cranked out electricity to light up those big houses. People were even stringing the lines to barns. A miracle—that's what it was. But only a few people had electricity, of course. One of them was Grandpa Smith over by Garden City. This hardworking German immigrant had built a house that ranked first in the community. The square white farmhouse was huge—twelve rooms in all. Sister Smith could draw water for her bath in an enameled bathtub that stood up off the floor on four lion's claw legs. She could actually choose between hot and cold water. And, they had another one of those bathrooms upstairs.

The new bishop, Ike Hartzler, and his family had a water tank in their attic. Water system. Bathroom. Wind-generated electricity. Batteries in the basement. But what the farmers liked best of all was that marvelous windmill on the top of the grainery that turned the hammermill, grinding whatever grains the men brought for grinding. Yes, they were making progress. Wouldn't it truly be a miracle if something happened to redeem them from the sticky mud that bogged down the buggy wheels when it rained? Only God knew the answer to that one. No one argued about one fact. If you got this Missouri mud on your shoes or boots and let it dry, fire and brimstone wouldn't blast it off.

Enough daydreaming. It was Thursday, and soon Twili and Mary Barb would arrive in the surrey with Cousin Samantha.

Her nieces were healthy girls. Mary Barb was getting near marrying age. And Twili? Only her quiet modesty and simplicity of spirit kept those muscular young farmers from pushing her into courting before she was sixteen.

Don't use the word, and don't mark anyone off as special, but Twili Yoder was just plain beautiful. No one would argue about that.

Chapter 2

Barbara heard their laughter as they turned the corner by the grainery. Her heart filled with joy as she anticipated the camaraderie and love of her nieces and meeting their visitor from the east, Samantha Hertzler.

She'd known Samantha's mother. Once years ago she and Salome had taken the train back to West Liberty for a funeral of one of their uncles and she'd met the Aaron Hertzlers, Samantha's parents.

In their church they kept the rules of order and wore plain clothes: cape dresses for all the sisters, and coverings made just according to the rule, square cornered and tied under the chin. Out here in Missouri, with folks coming from a half-a-dozen states, they weren't quite so strict.

"Samantha. You look just like your mother did at your age. Sixteen now, or thereabouts, aren't you?"

Barbara hurried down to the buggy stile to greet her nieces and their cousin. Might not get much work done with three giggling girls, but she'd show Samantha a hearty welcome and Christian fellowship.

Simon stepped up, wearing his straw hat with a bite out of the left side of the brim where old Timmon had sneaked up on him last week and bit off a chunk. He reached for the bridle of the horse, waiting for the girls to step out onto the stile.

"Auntie Barb and Cousin Simon!" Samantha descended from the buggy, followed by Mary Barb and Twili. They were bare-headed, hair parted in the middle. Mary Barb had wound hers tightly into a bun in the back. Twili's was braided and pinned around her head.

Their faces gleamed with health; broad smiles spread across their faces. Company always altered things and added spice. Except, why was Cousin Samantha so religious, always wearing her covering like that? And an old style, too.

Unlike Samantha, Mary Barb and Twili didn't wear capes on their dresses. Different communities, different customs. But things were plain too, here in the Mennonite churches in Cass County.

Barbara invited them all in to sit for awhile and have a cup of freshly-steeped mint tea. She passed a plate of her golden, sugar-coated snickerdoodles. It was peaceful there, with a gentle wind filtering through the screen of the back porch and the fragrance of the morning glories drifting in.

Twili and Mary Barb perched upon two rough, old bentwood kitchen chairs that had belonged to their grandmother, Sarah Yoder.

Samantha, little finger sticking straight out as she sipped her tea, cleared her throat and remarked, "Why, what ancient old chairs, Aunt Barb. Ought to get rid of those old eyesores." Then, lowering her cup and reaching for another snickerdoodle, her laughter rippled and rose up, drifting out through the screen and over the garden.

"Why, yes, child," Barbara sputtered, being a bit taken by the forward remark from her Ohio relative. "They're old chairs, real old chairs. The stories those chairs could tell, child."

"Momma would have thrown them out years ago. Back in Ohio we have a furniture store right in West Liberty. Momma just bought all new furniture." Samantha brushed her covering strings back and tossed her head.

"It is nice to have new things." Mary Barb joined in, wanting this visit and day of work at Aunt Barb's to flow smoothly. She felt obliged to throw in a few words. "I'd love to see your home someday, Samantha. I know it must be beautiful."

"Oh yes. Not like here at all. Our trees are taller than your trees. Momma always said a person couldn't raise flowers way out west in that God-forsaken Missouri with the heat coming down in the summer and scorching everything. You just ought to see our house shaded by those big oaks. Momma bought a new lavender couch since we got all hooked up with electricity. Auntie Barb, could I please have another cup of your tea? What kind of tea is it anyway? Momma says one ought to always drink Lipton's tea."

Twili put her cup down on the bench holding the potted begonias. She looked over at Mary Barb. What could she say to get in on the conversation? Why did Samantha have to talk all the time? "Well, Auntie Barb, we came here to work, so work we'll do. I'll sweep the carpets. Mary Barb likes to work in the bedrooms, change the beds, dust and straighten up. Samantha, would you care to help Mary Barb change and make the beds? Goes quicker when two work together."

"Don't you remember, Twili," Samantha replied. "I told you that bedroom dust and feathers make me choke up and sneeze. You and Mary Barb had better do the sweeping and dusting and bed changing. Aunt Barb, how can I help you?"

By this time Barbara saw that Samantha had her own plan for the day. She decided she'd be pleasant about it—maybe it wasn't going to be much of a fun day for Mary Barb or Twili either. Why, usually when those two come over here, we work 'till we drop and laugh until our sides ache. Barbara cleared her throat.

"Well, Samantha, I know just what you can help me

with. I'm going out to the garden to pick the last of the green peas. Maybe you can shell them there by that cool window in the kitchen."

That's how they began. Mary Barb strained her back reaching across those mattresses. She ran to the edge of the porch every few minutes to shake out the dust rag. Twili made the dust fly from Barbara's rag carpets as she pushed the Bissel sweeper—run by elbow grease—back and forth. Twili didn't mind the sweat beading on her brow. She was quick and lithe, and took after her grandmother, Sarah, who never knew when to quit.

The morning hours passed. Simon, freckles showing through his fair skin, hit the porch boards. He walked through to the little washroom off the pantry, picked up the bar of Lava soap and washed his hands, neck, and face in the little blue enameled basin. No need for a farmer boy to go through the entire house or climb those steps to use the bathroom. He'd save that for Wednesday and Saturday nights.

Aunt Barbara served some of the fresh picked peas from her garden, though it'd taken Samantha far too long to get them shelled. Hadn't her mother taught her how to work? She also boiled those new potatoes, serving them creamed. She'd hooked one of the young leghorn roosters by the leg, quickly twisted his neck, scalded and disemboweled him, cut him up, and tossed him in the skillet.

Nothing in the world smelled sweeter than Barbara Yoder's fresh fried chicken. Good thing Samantha was shelling peas and was spared seeing her wring the rooster's neck, based on how things had gone around here so far. She hated to think what Samantha might have said if she'd smelled those scalding, wet feathers.

Barbara called on Simon to lead in prayer. Then they ate.

Simon wasn't shy. He was a sensitive lad who took his faith and religion seriously. Now he'd assume his duty to help with the conversation here at Aunt Barbara's table. "Tell us about your church, Samantha."

"Our church is lots larger than yours out here in these sticks. Momma said she could never understand why some of her folks moved out here." Samantha cut one of the tasty new potatoes in half, sponged up the cream sauce with it, and popped it into her mouth. "Another thing, sisters of the church wear their coverings all the time. Why don't you folks wear your coverings all the time?" She sipped from her pressed glass water tumbler and stared at her cousins.

Twili and Mary Barb and their Aunt Barbara had remembered to put on their prayer coverings when they approached the table for this moment of prayer. But it was true that most of the sisters around here worked in their houses bareheaded. They only wore prayer coverings for church and for special times of prayer.

Simon, realizing that he had struck out on that one, didn't give up. He tried again. "What are the schools like in West Liberty?"

"We have a big new red brick school with steam heat. Three floors. Students are mostly from our church. I nearly fell out of the buggy laughing when Mary Barb drove by your schoolhouse up on that hill. How do you endure it?"

Then Simon made his biggest mistake. Turning to his aunt, an experienced farm woman, he said, "Auntie Barb, don't you think I'd better let the bull out of his pen so he can graze in that hay field?"

Mary Barb thought Samantha was going to swoon and fall off her chair. Her hand rose to her mouth and her eyes opened in horror as she glared at poor Simon. "Why, Simon Yoder! No one ever says that awful word around our house. (She meant, of course, the word *bull*). Why Father and brother Henry, if they have to ... I mean, if they talk at all about that ... they say 'the animal.'"

They tried their best to carry on a Christian conversation with Samantha, but they mostly struck out every time they opened their mouths.

Mary Barb washed up the dinner dishes and Samantha said she would be comfortable drying them. And, by the way, "Were they really planning to go to the singing tonight, and would there be many young gentlemen from the church there?"

All the young folks planned to go to the singing tonight. Even some of the middle-aged people with good voices who were skilled at reading the notes would be there. Music was important around here.

After she washed the dishes, Mary Barb decided she'd had enough of visiting and working with Samantha. Let Twili work with her. She'd go out to the washhouse, scrub the floor, clean up out there, and work off some of the tension that was building up within her.

The afternoon wore on. Samantha decided she'd rest awhile on the porch swing where it was shady. Twili asked her if she'd like to go upstairs to the back bedroom where Auntie Barb had her quilt frame set up and try her hand at working a little on that double wedding ring quilt. "I only crochet. I don't quilt, Cousin Twili," announced Samantha with a toss of her head.

Never before had Mary Barb scrubbed and swung the broom so hard. She even held her broom by the tip of the handle and ran it around the beams in the ceiling of the washhouse. When she finished cleaning, she planned to sort through Aunt Barb's glass fruit jars, arrange them according to size, and put them up on the shelves.

While Mary Barb swept the beams she noticed some sparrow nests up there. All the way around. She counted thirteen in all. "I'm going to get those dirty things out of there," she said to herself, putting down her broom and dragging over an old stool to stand on.

Mary Barb scraped and thrust with her outstretched

broom. Feathers and some straw drifted down on the blue scarf she'd tied around her head to protect her hair.

Good thing there were no baby sparrows in these nests. She couldn't stand the sight of those squirming, blind, naked, baby birds. Where would she put the bird nests? Burn them, that's what. But then she backed out of the washhouse door and the hot afternoon wind hit her. No. Better not burn sparrow nests on such an afternoon here at the edge of the garden. She could spread a dangerous fire that way.

Then Mary Barb noticed the old three-hole privy out by the garden. Why not stack the sparrow nests inside the privy? She could burn them another day. So that's just what she did. Stacked them up, thirteen high, in the corner of the privy. Was she ever glad to be finished with that job. Aunt Barb'd be pleased to see her washhouse so spick-and-span.

About four o'clock Samantha decided she needed to make a trip to the toilet. Things were so primitive here at Aunt Barbara's place. Who could believe it? There was a big bathroom upstairs, with a tub every bit as big as theirs at home. The water faucets had hot and cold water, that is in the winter when the big furnace downstairs was all heated up. Anyway, with all this, why hadn't that old-fashioned Barbara put in a flush toilet?

Samantha had to take herself out on the worn wooden sidewalk that led to the privy in the plum thicket. There was no way of getting around it and it humbled her considerably. What if she ran into a snake?

The day wore on. They did evening chores and ate supper: roast beef and mashed potatoes and gravy with rhubarb pie for dessert. Real tea, too. Tasted like her mother's Lipton tea.

Come twilight, cows lowed in the side pasture by the pond. Bob-o-links called and whippoorwills started their endless cries. The wind died down. Simon hooked up Hank and Timmon to the surrey and off they rode to Jacob Schrock's for the singing.

Must have been about forty-five people there. They cleared their throats and took their pitches. Singing from the *Harmonia Sacra,* the choruses ascended and rose out the open windows across the starry summer sky.

Faith and singing went together. How could one be a Christian and not sing about it? Young Simon's marvelous tenor rose up, supported by the richness of Eli Bontrager's vibrant bass. The hymns revealed Christ, the holy Savior. That's why they sang.

Samantha had a good voice, too. She enjoyed tipping her head to reach the highest notes. They would like to have her here all the time; they could use more clear sopranos like that.

They took a break from the singing and passed cookies and lemonade. Males blushed and visited with young females. Social custom and ritual. How else do people grow up and get paired off into marriages without forms and ways of doing things, without customs like singing school and Saturday night singings?

When they started singing again, Samantha just couldn't seem to sit still on her bench. Twili looked over at her cousin a second time. Yes, Samantha was twisting, wasn't she? Twili couldn't believe it, sophisticated Samantha letting go of one side of her hymnbook to scratch like that under her arm.

Whatever was bothering Samantha—as far as Twili was concerned—she had it coming, after the way she'd put them all down, going on and on like she'd done today, let alone letting them do most of the work.

Samantha had a very hard time holding that songbook and keeping her hands above her belt. Suddenly she squirmed too boldly for good manners.

There's a part in the chorus of "Master the Tempest Is

Raging" where you sing louder and louder, "No water can swallow the ship where lies the Master of ocean and earth and skies." Well, when they got to "skies," Samantha's fine soprano voice broke—away from note, staff, line, and even the page as it rose up in a wild screech, breaking the harmony. What on earth was wrong? It was becoming embarrassing.

As the evening drew to a close, Samantha's ungracious wiggling and screechy high notes got even worse. If the young men noticed it, she'd be shamed to death, that's for sure.

Even before they sang the last amen, Samantha was on her feet. Racing across the room to Simon she called, a wildness in her eyes, "Get the buggy, we've got to go. Hurry."

After what he'd been through with Samantha that day, Simon decided he wasn't going to let her keep on calling the shots. So Simon tarried, asking his male friends about how their corn was doing, and would they care to come over to the back pond some evening for a swim?

When Mary Barb saw tears beginning to slip down Samantha's cheeks, she interceded. "Bring up the surrey, Simon. We've got to take Samantha home. I believe she's getting sick."

Samantha never said a word on the ride home. Before she got to the buggy stile she leaped out and ran for the screen door. Barbara, startled by her sudden entry, jumped up. "Samantha, where are the rest? Where are you going?"

Samantha didn't even give notice that she'd heard. Jerking open the stairwell door, her feet sailed up the steps. "Bang!" went the bathroom door upstairs. Then Barbara heard the water running into her big tub.

By this time Mary Barb and Twili, worried and puzzled, had entered the dining room. What was wrong?

"I'll go up and see what's the matter. Poor child must have had an awful fright. Someone must have said something offensive to her." On tired legs Barbara slowly began to go up the steps.

"I'll come, too." Mary Barb followed after. So did Twili. "Poor Samantha. What is the matter?"

Samantha didn't seem to mind at all when Mary Barb, Twili, and Barbara knocked, then came on into the bathroom. They saw her dress, slip, underclothes, and stockings strewn across the floor as if she had been in a frenzy to free herself from them. Sitting in the big tub, in tears, Samantha cried, "Bugs, awful bugs."

Then they realized what was the matter. Eying a black stocking on the floor, Barbara spied the ugly little grey mites crawling and creeping. The sparrow nests! The sparrows were loaded with mites. Poor Samantha.

So the three of them ministered to their relative from Ohio, tenderly and lovingly bringing in the best soap and the best of their balms and oils. Barbara raced down the hall to get that new violet towel, soft and thick. Then she dipped her hand in the water and helped poor, humbled Samantha get rid of her mites.

When they finally got Samantha bathed, Twili and Mary Barb went into the bedroom and doubled over with laughter. They hooted and hollered. A part of them wanted to say, "She got what she deserved." But that was the sinful part. The other part of them knew they should bless Samantha, pray for her, treat her kindly.

The awful experience with the mites really did humble Samantha. Before she got on the train that would take her back to Ohio, she turned and told her relatives: "I've enjoyed my visit so much. You have been truly kind to me. Missouri is a beautiful state. I have to confess that I came here haughtily, feeling better than you. Well, I'm not. I love you, my cousins, and I'm going to plead with Father and Mother to send you tickets so you can come to Ohio next summer. I deserved those mites from those sparrow nests."

Then Samantha tipped her fine covering-crowned

head back and let out a long, healthy parting laugh. She waved good-bye as the steam engine chugged slowly down the track.

Chapter 3

Simon sat at the oak dining room table clasping the worn volume of *Josephus* he had borrowed from Preacher Daniel Yoder over at the Bethel Mennonite Church.

The scenes from ancient history captivated him. This brilliant historian from the time of Christ really knew how to bring the stories to life. Something grew within Simon's spirit: a hunger for more knowledge, the search of his own spirit for truth.

"Simon, it's time for a young farmer like you to get his rest." Barbara knew he was bone weary. But the eagerness of Simon's mind transcended the weariness of his lean body. His soul hungered for bread that is not of this world.

He read and loved his Bible. Simon was becoming aware that some were born for the tilling of the soil and for the harvesting of the grain, while others, perhaps like Daniel Yoder over at the Bethel Church, hungered for wisdom and knowledge. This hunger could at least be partially satisfied by more education.

"If you don't mind, Aunt Barb, I'd like to read awhile here by the lamp. My bedroom lamp upstairs doesn't give as bright a light. You're tired, Aunt Barb. Go on, get your rest."

Simon Yoder read until eleven o'clock, quenching his thirst for knowledge, opening his soul for wisdom. He'd been lying on his back in that big room upstairs with the blue cornflower wallpaper, wrestling with one thought lately, "Can I convince Father to let me go to high school?"

He remembered how guarded his people were about higher education. Modesty, humility—*gellassenheit*—it was called here. No one was better than another. One should not stand out in any prideful way. Education beyond the eighth grade signaled danger to the community, as an opening of the self to pride and worldliness.

Convincing Father to let me go to high school might be a struggle, thought Simon. What about Mary Barb? She was equally as bright as Simon. Could they dare push the question with Noah and Nettie? What about the preachers and the bishop of the church?

Simon first discussed his growing need for knowledge with his Aunt Barbara.

"I've always known, Simon, that the farm was not for you. You came here to help me after Salome married. I love you for it. You freely gave of yourself. I see with my own eyes how you struggle to do your work conscientiously. I'm proud of you. But, Simon, deep in my heart, I too have wished that you could go on to high school and then see where that leads. Talk to your father again. If you want me to, I'll say something to Noah and Nettie. I've got a lot of your grandmother Sarah in me. I remember one time when she hooked up the buggy and tore off over to Bishop Hartzler's to plead with him to be more understanding with your Uncle Seth when he and a lot of other young people could no longer keep up with his German sermons. Helped too. I believe I could ride over to Noah's and do the same."

Barbara chuckled, for she had a flashing vision of herself breaking that *gellassenheit* rule by driving over to Noah's in a cloud of dust, sitting behind the wheel of a shiny new Model T Ford, yellow wheels to boot.

But that was only a thought, a dream. Action had not

made it a reality. But, why not? What did her mother used to say about that Bible verse that was a great leveler? "There is neither male nor female." Why not show the sisters of the congregation that they too could learn to drive? Well, she'd see. Have to do something about it soon, the way it occupied her mind lately.

When Simon went home for the weekend, he found the courage to approach his father. "I want to go to high school. The farm is fine for Seth. You've always known we were different, Seth and me."

Noah agreed that all his children were special and different from each other. Seth was getting ready to rent the Aaron Hostetler place and strike out on his own; he was planning to marry Sonya Hershberger. They could work together, he and Seth, since the farms were adjoining. Plenty of youngsters around here waited to hire on as hands. He could manage. Barbara would have to take on another hand or two, too.

Then Preacher Noah remembered scenes that brought pain and sorrow to his heart. He'd brought it to the attention of the bishop and ministers. It was enough to sober them—truly a reflection that some kind of change was needed in their church. Two Sundays ago Shem Schrock and Adonis Bowman, lanky fourteen-year-olds weary of the long testimonials given by the three ministers and the bishop following his very own sermon, had slipped out the open window in the back of the packed, hot church building. They joined a small group of teenage boys gathered in the buggy shed swapping stories and whittling with their penknives. Shamefully, these boys had failed to come in to the service at all.

Yes, it was a grave matter. Then, too, Mennonites had started those colleges, two on the windswept prairies of central Kansas and the other planted thick in the middle of hundreds of Mennonites at Goshen, Indiana. Another in the Shenandoah Valley in Virginia. Some changes were needed.

St. Luke and the apostle Paul were highly-educated men, weren't they?

And what about Mary Barb? Noah'd been talking to Nettie about Mary Barb. She had discussed this high school business with her mother only a few days ago. It startled Nettie at first.

"Gracious, child, wouldn't that be learning the ways of the world—going to high school?"

"But Mother, there is so much to know. Times are changing. You know Cousin Samantha is going to high school back in Ohio. Several of her Mennonite friends go to high school."

"That's a big community, child. Care can be taken to make sure the teaching is in accordance with the Word. They probably have Mennonite teachers, too, who keep the doctrine of nonconformity to the world." After Samantha's visit here Nettie wanted to say, "Don't pattern yourself after Samantha," but she bit her tongue.

Then Nettie surprised Mary Barb with a big smile as she rose from her split willow rocker and laid aside her sewing. "I'll talk to Noah. We'll pray about it, Mary Barb. We want to be certain that it is the will of the Lord. You know if we let you go, we will be questioned by some. Your father, after all, is one of the ministers. Still, it would be nice to say, 'Mary Barb is a schoolteacher,' one of these days." She smiled serenely as she entered the kitchen.

Noah and Nettie prayed about it. Noah remembered his mother, Sarah, how she'd interceded for Seth that time he'd shamed himself by being so irreverent in church, cutting a nasty gash in his finger. Sarah had ridden over to the bishop and confronted him about the real problem. That had been an education problem too.

In the end, Barbara didn't have to buy that Model T with yellow wheels and come flashing into Noah and Nettie's place immodestly—maybe irreverently—jarring the very fine and accepted code of *gellassenheit*.

That fall both Seth and Mary Barb enrolled at the new high school in Garden City. Six others from the congregation joined them. No one would stand alone. Their people, plain in their dress, walked circumspectly, quietly, showing gentleness and kindness. Above all they did well in their studies and most importantly of all—they had their faith in Christ. A power greater than Simon, greater than Mary Barb, led them and their faithful parents. They only had to offer their spirits in openness and humility.

Getting to school and back wasn't easy. Noah had purchased an old, used buggy for them. Burtiss, an older horse but still energetic, pulled the buggy to Garden City through the dust in the fall and through the thick mud when it rained, over the frozen ruts or through the drifts when the ice and snow fell. And when the weather turned nasty for several days, they stayed the entire week at Esau Kenagy's place.

Soon, the greatest changes the community had ever experienced began to explode around them. Change happened—not only in the little community—but through the county, the state, the nation, even the world.

Black clouds of war swept over Europe, looming ugly with desolation, fear, and death. For some Mennonites of the little community it meant imprisonment and persecution. Soon, no one had much time to ponder whether or not it was sinful for six young folks to go to high school. They were occupied by far weightier matters.

On April 6, 1917, the United States declared war on Germany, entering the second bloodiest war the world had ever known. Nothing could surpass the death and destruction of the "War Between the States," but World War I came close. Though the United States fought in the conflict only nineteen months, the havoc and ruin that all wars bring reigned.

Sometimes it felt as if the wind sighed, "Woe unto you little community of Mennonites with your white meetinghouse, and others like you scattered through the Midwest and all through the East. For unto you will come the wrenching pangs. You will have an opportunity to give birth, not to a child as Sarah Yoder did during the Border Wars of the Civil War, but to give birth to faith, hope, and to the commitment to your pacifist faith."

Within a month hysteria broke loose.

"What is this leaflet passed to me on the streets of Garden City today," said farmer Timothy Schwartz, with a worried look on his face. "From the Creel Committee. Here, Brother Hartzler." Shaking, he put it in the outstretched hand of the bishop.

Bishop Hartzler surveyed it, his greying beard tipped toward his chest as he squinted, dipping his head for better light.

"Hate mail. That's what it is. Hate mail against any German people. Warnings against aliens and persons of German birth, pacifists, and socialists. They will all be targets of the local committees of safety. Whatever that is. Doesn't sound like a safety committee to me. 'The Kaiser, the Beast of Berlin.' God help us."

Soon came the announcement that all eligible men from eighteen to thirty-eight were to be drafted into the army. The news shook the nation and jarred this little community of those who sought peace, who farmed the land with diligence, and who followed Christ with faithfulness.

The ministers and the bishop held a meeting after Sunday service for the worried men of the congregation. "If you are drafted, state your position as a follower of Christ. State it clearly. Under no circumstances should we enlist as soldiers and fight. Choose rather to suffer affliction and persecution than to inflict violence upon others." They were not yet aware that even giving such counsel was a seditious act.

Ignorance swept the land and many young men began an ordeal of suffering together. These young men, trained from their mothers' bosoms and the hands of their fathers that "thou shalt not kill" and "if anyone strikes thee on the cheek, turn to him also the other," would experience bewilderment and confusion. They didn't fully understand that the majority of young men would laugh at such seemingly foolish ideas.

Vigilante groups roamed the countryside, armed with shotguns and rifles. The United States Congress passed the Sedition Act, which supported the hysteria against those of German tongue and birth, let alone those who could not take up arms because of their faith and conscience.

"Food in German-owned markets is poisoned," rang the cry from town to town, soon bankrupting those grocers whose misfortune happened to be that they had a German accent, went to a German-speaking church, or belonged to the Mennonites or Dunkers. One could be held for questioning, according to the Sedition Act, for conversing in German with a friend. What would happen to Ida Yoder and Sara Hooley, who talked in Pennsylvania Dutch on the phone daily? Would they be dragged up as aliens?

Weekly, things became worse. Captions in the county papers ran wild against all people of German origin—all were suspected of sedition. There was wide objection to German music. Entertainers with German names were suspect, as were teachers of German language in high schools. Overnight, sauerkraut became known as "liberty cabbage," and frankfurters as "liberty pups."

On April 19, 1917, the *Cass County Democrat* published: "No longer are there jingoes and pacifists, extremists either for or against the entry of the United States into the World War. No, there is not now in the country room for even that detestable brand of citizen known as the 'straddler' or 'middle of the roader.' The die has been cast—citizens are now either patriots or traitors, loyal Americans or cowards."

The die was cast. War hysteria began to push young men into the molds for war.

Chapter 4

Seth bowed his head in shame and pity for Hollis Troyer and Benjamin Eicher, who said they couldn't wait to be drafted and get to France.

Hollis had never joined the church. He never gave any evidence that he heard the Spirit of God breathe near him. He patterned himself after his father, Esau J., who drove his sad-faced wife and three daughters to the meetinghouse about once a month. Esau J. and Hollis were among those who gathered out at the far end of the horse barn, passing around their tobacco plugs, letting their minds wander upon the things of this world; things far away from building up the spirit.

The holy words and sacred songs rose up like the anthems of angels, sweeping out of the open meetinghouse windows, and—sadly—over the closed doors of their hearts.

Benjamin Eicher was different. He was a sensible fellow, but a little too lighthearted. Seth couldn't remember Ben being serious about anything unless it was the day he had to shoot his riding horse when it broke its leg jumping a ditch in the alfalfa field. Ben had been baptized with Seth, but for Ben it had been only a formality, a ritual. He did it because it was the thing to do. Like the seeds in the parable that fell upon the thin soil and rocky places, Ben's faith barely sent down roots before it withered at the top.

BERLIN MENNONITE CHURCH

Letha Harshbarger's public confession at communion time of her pregnancy, and Ben's absence and irresponsible behavior toward Letha, brought about his excommunication. Sad. Such breaks should be spanned over by penitence and confession, by sorrow of the soul, so that the spirit can be renewed by the loving grace of Christ. The apostle Paul said that sin must not abound just so that grace could abound.

Barbara had made her monthly trip to Garden City for needed staples and a piece of calico cloth. She forgot herself and slipped into Pennsylvania Dutch when she responded to Annie Swartzentruber, who'd been so glad to see her and had opened up the conversation in Dutch. They shared what common women of the prairie lands share: how the blackberries were ripening, how the tomatoes needed rain. Then Annie began to tell her worries about her grandson, Ned, and how he might have to sign up for the draft.

Walter Happersall, the grocer, interrupted. Sternly, with his glasses down over his nose, he peered above the two women. He pointed with his long finger at the newly-painted sign above the counter where the two Mennonite women stood. "Speak English Only in Here" read the black letters outlined in red.

Shocked, Barbara returned Walter's stern stare. "Walter, I've paid my taxes regularly, year after year on my place, never late. I've been buying my staples from you since back in '95, and you have the nerve to put up a sign like that? *Ich bin enteuscht in dich!* (I'm disappointed in you!")

As the women left the store, Annie grew afraid. She thought of her grandson and what might happen to him. The letter she had received from her cousin Peter Miller out in Protection, Kansas, gave her cause to be wary. Unsympathetic vigilantes of the community had painted his barn yellow. Even worse, three or four of them walked in on their Sunday worship service and in front of the whole congregation, nailed a big American flag on the wall of the meetinghouse. Annie was cautious and afraid for her people.

Ruby Horst, not having a telephone in her house, thought she'd stop in at the Clearfork Telephone Company to use the public phone to call her cousin Esther. She had to visit with Esther, staring straight at a sign reading, "Speak English Only on the Telephone." It gave Ruby goose bumps.

On June 5, 1917, Seth and two of his faithful friends from his Sunday school class, Aaron Kenagy and Eli Bender, plus Ben Eicher and Hollis Troyer, drove over the dusty road and up big Kohler Hill. They were on their way to Harrisonville to obey the law of the land and register for the draft.

Seth, Aaron, and Eli were prepared to declare their position regarding war. They had prayed about it; they trusted God. Like Peter and John in the New Testament, they believed the Holy Spirit would provide the words for their tongues to utter in the needed time.

Lottery numbers were drawn on July 20 in Washington, D.C. Each number pulled from the lottery applied to a registrant in counties throughout the nation. Mothers anguished, and gasps could be heard across the land.

By late summer draft board clerk Gilleland had sent notices to 312 registrants in Cass County to report for a physical examination. If they passed, they were bound for Camp Funston, near Junction City, Kansas.

Seth and Aaron were both chosen in the first lottery. They had two days to pack a valise with clothes, toothbrushes, soap, and razors. God only knew the future—where they would be taken, what they would need. They had affirmed that they would not wear the uniform of the American army. President Wilson's decree that those objecting to military service for conscience' sake and who were already baptized members of peace churches would serve in noncombatant roles calmed their fears somewhat.

What worried Aaron and Seth, though, was that *non-*

combatant hadn't been defined. Just what did it mean? Before the months ahead were over, they found out that they were not the only ones confused about it.

They had a Saturday and the blessed Sunday to prepare. Throwing a few clothes into a bag was a matter of little consequence. What mattered was the condition of their spirits.

The Sabbath service and being with the brothers and sisters of the congregation soothed like the blessed balm of Gilead applied to their souls. Seth closed his eyes and absorbed the rhythms and vibrations of the heavenly singing: "My Jesus, as thou wilt; Oh, may thy will be mine; Into thy hand of love I would my all resign."

What do people without faith do—people like Ben Eicher, now outside the holy fellowship, and Hollis Troyer, who said that he never heard the call of God? How do they live? What illusions they must follow in seeking after pleasure.

Seth gave thanks for his faith and for his roots, for his dear preacher father, and his pious mother sitting there on the sisters' side of the congregation. Today, Nettie's peaceful face was touched by the weight of what Ben and Seth faced. She too prayed from the secret place of her heart, "My Jesus, as thou wilt."

Black-coated and white-bearded Bishop Hartzler lifted up his voice in eloquent reading of the holy Scripture. He read the comforting testimony of faith: "Lord, thou hast been our dwelling place in all generations. Before the mountains were brought forth, or ever thou hadst formed the earth and the world, even from everlasting to everlasting, thou art God.... Establish thou the work of our hands upon us."

When the service ended and Seth and Aaron had received the holy kisses of their brethren, and with the prayers for them ringing in their hearts, Seth walked through the front doors of the white meetinghouse. He stood in the grove of giant sycamore trees that offered their own praises to God above. The beauty around him—the pastures, the wild honeysuckle and rose, the sweep of the prairie winds, the endless billows of drifting clouds—all proclaimed the glory of God.

Seth had driven his own buggy to church, for afterward he wanted to drive Sonya Hershberger back with him for Sunday dinner and family fellowship. Engaged to be married, they had decided to postpone the wedding. "Surely the war will not last long."

The buggy wheels rumbled over the planks of the wooden bridge as willow fronds reached out and sighed as they passed. Mourning doves called, announcing the possibility of an evening shower.

Seth, taking the reins in his right hand, reached over with his left hand and held Sonya's long, thin fingers. "You must write me as soon as I know where I'll be staying."

"I'll miss you so, Seth. Our hopes and our dreams ... postponed, put off. Not only ours, but the dreams of hundreds of others."

"We have our faith. We have the Lord." A lump crept up in Seth's throat. A tear streamed down Sonya's cheek. She took her handkerchief, wiped her eyes, and brushed back the strings of her prayer covering. They rocked on, down that road every thinking person must take, that road of contemplation and decision making. How blessed they were, for they did not make their choices alone. The Lord gave them wisdom, guidance, remembrance: "I will be with you until the end of the age."

Chapter 5

Back they went to that town on the hill, once called Fort Harrisonville during the Civil War. Back to the place where Grandmother Sarah Yoder, trying to obey Order Number Eleven, found herself engulfed in a hell where civil law had been abandoned. Back to the place where that dear old slave woman, Marianne, had fallen dead from a drunken soldier's rifle shot.

Seth prayed, "Lord, show me the way." Strangely, a calmness overcame him through the rough and tumble of the day. He got a lot of odd looks when he mentioned to the officer that he was a conscientious objector and could not perform military service. Six of them, four Mennonites and two from the Dunker church, had said that. Youthful, clean shaven, they stood out with their dark trousers and plain shirts without ties. Some other registrants recognized them. "There go two flat-headed Dutchmen," called Harley Single from over by Gunn City, pointing with a dirty finger.

"How many times do you dunk a Dunker?" sneered Woodey Heavener, spitting his tobacco juice towards the brass spittoon.

"What does this mean on your card, 'Conscientious Objector'?" boomed the heavyset intake officer. He hunched forward, grasping the card with two hands as if he had a seditious and dangerous felon in front of him.

"My conscience cannot permit me to enter military service or wear the uniform of any army. I am a Mennonite; it is our faith. It is the way I believe Christ would have me take." Seth stood straight, his dignity still about him, clothed yet in his civilian clothes and draped in spirit by these words of comfort.

"Bang!" went the officer's hand, stamping Seth's card. "Move on down the line for your physical." Why did he have to be so loud? Ben Eicher stepped up next, as Seth headed toward the line waiting to go down the street to the armory for their physical examinations. If they passed, they would have another much more taxing examination at the camp of their destination.

Herded into a room in the armory, they were ordered to take off all their clothes. Seth, Ben, and Aaron, among the young men of various ethnic backgrounds and differing religions, took off their shoes and socks, then completely disrobed.

Pained, almost shocked, they stood: young male farmers, swaying, lifting their feet to maintain balance, naked before each other. Seth was only getting a foretaste of what was to come. The odor of sweat rose up in the overheated building.

"Ain't that one of them Mennonites up yonder without his Dutchman's breeches on?" a raspy voice jeered from the line behind Seth somewhere. "One of them yellow-bellied objectors," spat Harley Single. Seth felt the jab of a fountain pen in his back. He staggered. Naked, sweating, his heart rate increased. "My Jesus, as thou wilt," he prayed silently, thinking of the Savior who hung naked on the cross. This day, too, would pass. "I am safe when thou art nigh."

Behind him, Seth heard coarse and vulgar comments about his body. His stomach turned.

There were added humiliations. Three separate doctors raised up from their stools, tapping chests, listening to the young lungs and beating hearts. Strange hands reached out, grasping private parts of their bodies. Seth did not flinch; he looked straight ahead. Then he was asked to bend over in a most humiliating position as his body was invaded by the hand of the physician. "Cough," came the doctor's order.

After donning their clothes, Seth, Ben, and the others joined the crowd of recruits for the instructions from the troop commander who would escort them by train to Camp Funston.

Ben Eicher, the excommunicated Mennonite, failed to pass his physical. "Eyesight. Why he wouldn't be able to shoot nothing," growled the doctor. And Hollis Troyer? Hollis, wild-eyed, whooped for joy upon discovering he'd passed. He strutted down the sidewalk to join the crowds gathered on the square, showing off his muscular build and tipping his hat at the passing girls who were seeking to befriend the soldiers. Ben simply headed for the nearest saloon to await the further glorious events of the day.

Seth and Aaron, fatigued by the ordeal, walked over to the pine trees on the lawn of the courthouse to rest awhile and to get their bearings. The afternoon sun pierced a cloud bank.

They talked about home and how blessed they'd been, with kind fathers and mothers and a Christ-centered faith. They had received teachings week after week at the meetinghouse, through prayers at the family table, and in the kindnesses shown them through the years. They'd experienced forgiveness for their follies. Grandmothers like Sarah had loved them and had interceded to the bishop for them. They pondered in silence, these Mennonite youth, and when their hearts were full of thankfulness, they began to sing together as their spirits healed from the onslaughts of the day.

> Awake my soul, to joyful lays,
> And sing thy great Redeemer's praise;
> He justly claims a song for me,
> His loving kindness, oh, how free!
> Loving kindness, loving kindness,
> His loving kindness, oh, how free!

Before the train filled with young men from southwestern Missouri arrived, many of the recruits sang, too. They mingled and shoved through the crowds, reveling in the extravagant sendoff party.

War, after all, is unpalatable without the proper dressing. Gathering on church grounds in the town, local clergy led in prayers. Town dignitaries and officials gave speeches and exhortations. One prominent businessman opened up the private club in the back of his business establishment for the newly recruited soldiers. Wine and liquor flowed, permitting the many selves that lurk within to march without sensitivity over frightful places where they would otherwise not tread.

Theater owners gave out free passes to the movies. Marvelous screen pictures captivated onlookers and dulled their sensibilities. Pleasure and patriotism, dished out by the elders, sugar-coated the more ghastly aspects of the great, bloody war blasting Europe.

The hotel hosted free dinners for this milling crowd of smiling, cheering young men who had learned patriotic songs at the concert at the south end of the courthouse. Songs occupied the mind, so thoughts could not focus upon the real needs of the soul or the tragic issues at hand.

Good-bye, Ma; Good-bye, Pa,
Good-bye mule with the old hee-haw.
I may not know what the war's about
But I'll bet, by gosh, I'll soon find out.
And oh, my sweetheart, don't you fear
I'll get you a king for a souvenir
I'll get you a Turk and a Kaiser too
And that's about all one feller can do.

When the first pink of morning tinted the eastern sky, the wailing of the night train swept over their heads. The cool, easterly wind foretold a truer message about their destination and what the winds of war really bring.

Chapter 6

Back in the little community, folks adjusted their minds and spirits. They changed their working patterns and schedules to fill the gaps left by the young men who had been drafted. Autumn seemed to bring only dreary clouds and rain, and mud everywhere. The grey fog engulfing the land lay like the shrouds of cannon smoke over dreary battlefields. All the world was at war.

Noah would not stop Simon from continuing high school. His son made superb marks. The principal had called him in and told him, "Your son is destined for a high calling. Only once before have we had so bright and serious a student."

Mary Barb did well, too. The mud bogging down their buggy wheels, the drenching, cold rains, the stresses of staying in Garden City when they couldn't make it home, doing what labors they could for their keep—none of this could dampen their spirits.

Education and a chance to go to school, what more could young people ask for? They had endured some slurs and taunts, especially since the draft began. But they remembered the stories in the *Martyrs Mirror,* how their people were humiliated, insulted, persecuted, and even burned and drowned for their faith. They counted it all as joy, these minor slurs. "There goes that Dutch broad. Now I know where they got the name for that flat-headed cabbage."

Once a muscular bully, Harris Tar, two years older than Simon, detained him in the washroom of the high school. "Hear your brother's one of them conscientious objectors," Harris sneered. Simon was startled. A trickle of fear descended from his neck downward as the young farmer's hands grabbed him by the shirt collar.

"Hey, Tolbert. Come here." He shouted coarsely to a lanky, pimple-faced teenager opening the door of the toilet stall.

"Yoder, it's too bad we ain't out on your stinking kraut farm so we could stick your head right down in that privy hole. Nobody could ever tell the difference anyway. Red hair fits right in with what's piled up down at the bottom of the privy. Only thing me and Tolbert can do here is to dunk your kraut head in one of these flush stools. Tolbert, did you get your bowels emptied yet there in the stall? Wouldn't want to put this kraut head in an empty toilet bowl, would we?"

God intervened. Mr. Bolden, the principal, entered the washroom at that moment. Harris dropped his hand from Simon's perspiring neck and lowered his eyes sheepishly as the fierce black eyes of Mr. Bolden focused upon him. "Trouble here, Harris?"

Other episodes happened, but these young people, looked upon as naive and simple, really believed that verse in the Bible: "Blessed are they which are persecuted for righteousness sake; for theirs is the kingdom of heaven."

Then one day Sonya Hershberger received a two-page letter from Camp Funston. Sonya, who had been helping her mother peel and cut up the apples for canning, could scarcely contain herself. She'd checked with the Yoders at the meetinghouse, but they hadn't heard from Seth yet.

Seth gave her details about Camp Funston, located 140 miles west of Kansas City where the Smoky Hill and Republican rivers run together and form the Kansas River.

Built on the bottomlands of the Kaw in the east part of the Fort Riley military reservation, the barracks and administrative buildings rose up to meet the full force of the prairie winds. Temperatures ranged from 115 degrees in the summer to thirty-two below when bitter winter winds swept over the plains.

We Mennonites are placed in detention camps, and so far have not been required to wear the uniform. Seth didn't tell her that one reason they didn't wear uniforms was that the uniforms hadn't yet arrived, so the camp commander had requested blue overalls for everyone.

At first there had been a kind of general confusion. President Wilson was slow in defining just what conscientious objection meant. Later they found out that he meant conscription into the army with service in noncombatant units—construction, medical, engineering.

Local policy, bias, imagination, or whatever else seemed to work determined how officials treated objectors. Camp Funston garnered the most infamous reputation for treatment of these young men.

Things were confusing here at first. I did pass my physical here, it was long and detailed. Seth didn't write that it was painful; that he had been punched and prodded. Running to the rescue of an Amish youth who'd been tripped by a sneaky recruit, a sergeant had grabbed him roughly and threatened him with detention in the guardhouse if he didn't mind his business. Who did he think ran this war anyway—yellow-bellied Mennonites or real men like the sergeant himself?

After the week of general confusion, some of us Mennonites decided that we would go to the commander and tell him we could provide some service. So, at present, five of us have been assigned to the hospital, three to the kitchen, and the rest to the sanitation department. I am doing well, I have a faith that sustains me. Now I know why children should memorize Bible verses. How they help me! If I have a bad moment, I can endure the pain with the comfort of the blessed verses.

Seth didn't tell her of the beatings that had occurred in the confusion or about the Holdeman Mennonites who had been thrown into the prison cell block. Beaten and ridiculed, their beards had been jerked from their young faces.

We Mennonites have to understand how confusing this is for the camp commanders and other officers. Some of them try to do their duty. We are seen as a great, confusing bother. Worse, they believe the greatest danger lies in that we might convert the soldiers to our views.

So, the screws tightened on Quakers, Mennonites, Brethren, and others. The officials viewed these conscientious objectors—people of German descent—as seditious, as people who might spread propaganda.

Finally, in October 1917 the War Department endorsed a policy: "Make them disappear. Expose them to excitement, to a barrage of patriotism, to the *esprit de corps* of the army. Ignore all their objections. In other words, convert them to the military mind."

Such tactics didn't work at Camp Funston. A few of the regular draftees, wearing military uniforms, pleaded to the officers about the treatment some of the Mennonites received. This made matters worse quickly.

Then came new commands regarding the objectors: "Break down their morale. Give them orders that are contradictory, so they cannot obey. Then throw them into the guardhouse."

Seth and Aaron drew sanitation duty. The fact that a group of civilians from town had been employed for the same work allayed some of their fears. Mixing these objectors and the citizens together made the pickup of garbage and cleaning of toilets work that they could do without a violation of their principles.

But then the army withdrew the civilians, leaving the sanitation work completely in the hands of the objectors. The army made the announcement publicly: "This sanitation work is an essential part of our military operation."

"I could not do it, neither could Aaron." Seth later told his little Missouri community. "We simply could not do something that was essential for a war machine.

"Courts-martial began. More imprisonments in the guardhouse followed.

"A group of Mennonite men who could not comply with their orders had to march to their quarters. Their refusal to work had angered a group of regular recruits. These angry men attacked the Mennonites as they marched along. They pushed some of the conscientious objectors against tree trunks and beat them in their stomachs and faces. Others got knocked to the ground and became fair game for two or three who pounced on them.

"General Leonard Wood feared an uprising in the camp. He also feared some of the soldiers might stage a mass defection to the detention camps to join the objectors. Tension mounted.

"In November, I remember the cold, icy rain. They forced five of us, Mennonites all, to stand outside our barrack all day long without anything hot to drink, and with no food. Some fell over from exhaustion. Finally, we got to eat some soup and to sleep in our bunks. Suddenly, in the depths of the night the lights came on. They ordered us to get up and go to the shower room. There, burly officers hooked up hoses and turned them on us. Ben Hartzler stood in the corner to keep from falling. They kept the hose on his head until he collapsed. This was to break down our morale, our beliefs.

"Our ministers wear the plain coat, so they mistook them as priests and forbade them to enter the camp for fear they would spread sedition among the Germans."

A month later Seth wrote: *I cannot receive any church papers. The* Gospel Messenger *of our church is looked upon as propaganda that spreads sedition and German alliances.*

One of their ministers, Timothy Cooprider, finally managed to get into the camp to visit three young men from his congregation. To the dismay of the little community in Missouri, Brother Cooprider later wrote: *A number of our men have been court martialled and sent either to Alcatraz or Fort Leavenworth. They report that terrible things occur there. Our innocent men are victimized, deprived of food and water, and thrown into cold dungeons. They are forced to march in freezing rain. God help us.*

Seth and Aaron received the opportunity to eat of the same bread that their forbears had eaten. They had been hounded, persecuted, placed in dungeons, and burned at the stake.

The letter continued: *Somehow—I do not know how—but midst it all, I have a great peace in my heart. Prayer never came so easily, and the presence of Christ seems so real. Those tortures and treatments of shame only remind me of the blessed Christ, and the pain and suffering actually becomes the very point at which the peace of Christ enters.*

The drive to buy war bonds to finance the war reached a heated pitch. Despite the pressure, most in the little community did not buy the war bonds, but gave large gifts to relief agencies or to the Red Cross. "What shall we do?" asked Bishop Ike Hartzler's congregation. No clear answer came. Some left rather large sums in banks for a period of months, which allowed other bank monies to be released to support the war.

Then the Ku Klux Klan surfaced, much as it had back in the awful war that Grandma Sarah Yoder had survived. A wave of terror rippled from one edge of the little community to the other, driving them to their Bibles, to their knees, to the love and support of one another, and to the strengthening of their faith. Reigns of terror sometimes offer these opportunities—provided that body and spirit are not rent asunder.

Chapter 7

Bishop Hartzler left the community for three days, assisting a church in northeastern Missouri. Mary, his wife, and her little daughter, Dorcas, a pudgy four-year-old, stayed alone in their big farmhouse.

At first they heard soft murmurings, like the wind in the eaves. It continued, getting louder. Then Mary heard the wrenching of the yard gate from its hinge and saw the ugly flash of a torch held high. Her heart froze in terror when she saw that a tall man wearing a white robe held the torch. The peaked hat of the Klan rose up into the swirling smoke. Two holes stared at her window from the mask and wind-flapped robe.

Then she saw four or five other robed men sink a post. No, it wasn't a post. It looked like a cross. They planted a tall cross coated with pitch right there in her front yard.

Suddenly the torchbearer lit the cross, which flamed up, lighting the front side of her house and all of the yard. Twenty or so robed Klansmen grouped, facing her porch, their fearful costumes flapping in the wind.

"Oh, merciful God, have pity upon me," she prayed. Little Dorcas, awakened by the noise and the light, ran to her mother, clinging to her skirt. She did not cry.

Mary felt that the wall would cave in, so hard did the Klansman pound at her door. She brushed back a wisp of hair and her covering strings and marched to the door. God alone gave her strength.

As she opened the door, the tall, white-clad Klan leader rushed to stand in the doorway. He jeered at her. "Old Mennonite lady, where's your war bonds? We want to see your war bonds. Look here, fellers, the old German broad's whelped a pup." He pointed to the frozen-faced child.

Two others joined the fearful, white-clothed demon on her porch. The shorter one, with a voice that Mary said later she was sure she recognized, whispered raspingly, "Better spread some tar under her nose."

Then, the awful group, given over to the works of Satan, drifted away from her yard to their cars or whatever vehicles they'd used for transportation. The grotesque and devilish caravan snaked through the little community, threatening the innocent.

Barbara's brother Noah, a faithful minister, had been warned two days before by the blacksmith, Curley Boiles. He was a muscular, hardworking, kind man who befriended the Mennonites and especially appreciated Noah and Nettie and their family.

"I heard some talk, Noah. Maybe you ought to know about it. Couple of rednecks around here, certainly not your friends," the blacksmith wiped the sweat from his brow with his hairy arm, "said they were going to get them some tar. They mentioned your place." Then Boiles turned back to the sorrel horse and his shoeing.

Noah and Nettie were known through the greater part of the county as people of Christian faith. Their integrity gleamed like sunlight reflecting from the metal blades of the windmill. If someone's house burned down in the night, Noah and Nettie appeared with a basket of canned goods and a smoked ham. Sister Nettie always had three spare quilts or comforters made by her own hands to give out to the poor and needy. No one could fault their Christian commitment or their quiet goodness.

Noah didn't rightly know what to do. He had heard about these kind of threats. He'd read in the church papers that this had happened in other Mennonite communities, but thought maybe it was only a rumor. He didn't tell Nettie or Twili or Mary Barb. Simon was over at Aunt Barb's helping her with the spring hay. Everyone knew Seth was out in that detention camp in Kansas. Why frighten others? Besides, it might not come about.

Brother Noah decided to trust the Lord he'd followed all these years. He thought of the blessed Christ and his betrayal, even by the chosen disciples, and the words of comfort from the Gospel: "Blessed are ye when men revile you and persecute you...."

Since it was late spring, the frogs raised a shrill chorus by the farm pond. Young cattails pushed through the water, gently rippling in the evening breeze. A few clouds swept over the moon, now and then. There was light, then shadow.

Nettie had retired to the bedroom. Mary Barb and Twili sat upstairs reading and sewing. Noah was tired from planting corn with his new planter, the one hooked up to a wire that dropped the grains of corn as regularly as the ticking of a clock.

He comforted his heart by reading that Bible passage in 2 Kings where the king of Israel was troubled because of the attacks of the Syrians, and how the Syrians descended upon the camp of Elisha. Completely surrounded by the Syrian army, Elisha's servants feared, wondering what to do. "Fear not, for those who are with us are more than those who are with them," Noah read.

Elisha prayed that his servant might have open eyes in order to see. When the servant opened his eyes, behold: "The mountain was full of horses and chariots of fire round about Elisha."

After asking God to strike the Syrians with blindness,

Elisha then delivered the entire band of Syrian soldiers to the Israelites. The king of Israel asked the question too often harbored in the hearts of people: "My father, shall I slay them?"

Elisha answered, "You shall not slay them. Would you slay those whom you have taken captive with your sword and with your bow? Set bread and water before them, that they may eat and drink and go to their master."

These words comforted Noah's tired body and soul; even here in the Old Testament he'd found a rich illustration of nonresistance. Now he could go to bed.

An hour later, if you were not asleep and if you listened carefully, you would have heard the murmur of motors—the mingling of Ford and Chevrolet truck and car motors. Ghostly shadows loomed up in the moonlight out by the road flanked by evening primroses. Lights had been turned off for the last mile or so. They parked the vehicles as quietly as possible. Doors opened and closed softly as they attempted to keep down the noise.

A motley crowd rose up in the shadowy moonlight, like ghouls rising from an open trench in the earth. Sounds of muffled laughter drifted in the wind. The intoxicating smell of honeysuckle on the fence mingled with the heavy, noxious odor of tar.

Walter Happersall—the same one Barbara spoke to in German the day he'd tacked up that sign in his grocery store—led the shifting group of men. His lanky arm held a bucket of tar. Others raised brushes gleefully.

Through the soft dust of the lane they came, weaving and bobbing. A whiskey bottle passed from Harris Tar back to Bodie Spank. Ribald laughter broke out, carried forward on the evening wind.

Old Tibbon, the cattle dog, raised up. He'd been taught not to bite human beings, not to jump on them. He did, however, begin to bark loudly and jump up on the yard fence. Frightened by the vagabond crew descending on his master's farm, his hackles rose at the smell of the strangers.

Noah, awakened from the night's first deep sleep, looked out the window to see why Tibbon was carrying on like that. Had the bull gotten out? Nettie awakened, too, and rolled out of her side of the bed. She padded over to the window; two long braids cascaded down her back.

Then, a torch flared. The crowd lingered in the shadows of the weeping willow and the maple trees. Cowards do not want to be seen in the light of the sun or of the evening moon. Bodie Spank tied his red handkerchief over his nose and held up the pine torch. Murmurs grew as his followers tied dirty rags and red handkerchiefs over their faces.

"We're huntin' yellow bellies tonight, Noah, and according to our records you surely qualify. Get yourself down here."

A tide of ugly jeering and booing rose up toward Noah and Nettie.

"Oh, merciful heaven. Noah, don't go down there." Nettie clung to her husband. She was weeping, trembling. "What if they set fire to the house?" She thought of her young, innocent daughters upstairs in their room and nearly fainted.

The jeering grew louder. Jake Slaughter had silenced poor old Tibbon with a blow from a limb he'd picked up in the lane.

"Gonna paint over the yellow belly!" screamed the crowd. The ghouls began to dance and stagger in the broken shadows. Liquor raced through their blood. A bottle crashed and broke into pieces as it hit the side of the house. Walter Happersall quickly opened another from the supply he'd brought along in his gunnysack.

"I have to go down. Maybe they will listen to reason."

But there is no reason in a crowd, a crowd intoxicated not only by spirits but the false intoxication that comes from pouncing upon the less fortunate and poor, the alien with different facial features, the religious with beliefs that, to them, seemed scandalous.

Walter Happersall, his mind frenzied by the liquor he'd drunk, turned to his cronies. "You all need more fortification?" He dug in his sack for a big bottle of bourbon. He uttered coarse and vulgar words, swearing, "You all can't paint yellow bellies without proper fortification!" His wild laughter rose in the wind.

Then Claude Fitzbottom remembered that this flat-headed Dutch farmer had two young daughters who wore those funny little black bonnets and even worse, those white caps. But before thought carried the vulgar train to something heinous, poor Noah came through the front door, hooking his overall straps over his underwear.

"Whoooooeeeeeee!" whooped the drunken crowd. "Did you ever see such knock knees? But, what did you expect from a yellow belly Dutchman?" sneered Hollis Dunn, taking a hearty swig from the bottle of bourbon.

The vulgarities got worse. Each part of Noah's body received a particular crude insult, too jarring to mention.

Noah faltered, cleared his throat, and spoke. "Neighbors, whoever you are, what do you want?"

Jeers and hoots rose up to the heavens. Charlie Bothers lifted his arms and shouted, "Bring us out your war bonds, Yoder. Show us your bonds. Ain't allowing any slackers go by without being taken notice of." A devilish laugh ascended to the treetops.

"Neighbors, I wish I could see you better. I'd have you all in. Put on some coffee. Sit awhile and talk together. I think you know that I do not have any war bonds."

"Grab the traitor." Silas Woser and Pawdy Doone needed no further command. They raced to the stoop, grabbing Noah by the shoulders. Pawdy had his arm clenched around Noah's throat.

"Bring up the tar." Walter Happersall's voice carried

loudly in the night air. Noah recognized the voice, and his heart sank.

"Why, Walter Happersall, what are you doing here?" Pawdy had released his brutal hold on Noah's throat, so he could utter words and breathe. "Nettie was just in your store today and you sacked up six dollars worth of groceries for her."

Thud! Burt Wilson, tired of the slowness of the whole procedure, slammed his fist into Noah's face. Why waste time? Time to dunk or paint, wasn't it? What had they come here for anyway? Who wanted to sit around and pass the time of day with sissies and yellow bellies? Blood began to stream from Noah's broken nose.

So five of the staggering, intoxicated raiders dragged Noah out by the yard gate in the full moonlight. As they tore off his overalls and underwear, hoots and laughter rose up like frightened crows from a dank swamp. Curses and swears mingled with insults at his naked body.

"The tar. The tar, stupid." Groceryman Happersall, the liquor getting to him, changed moods. Angrily he hollered at Burt Wilson, "Get the brushes going. What do you think we came here for?"

The brush slapped and swished hot tar into Noah's thick grey hair. Hot tar dripped into his eyes and spread across his face, and down his neck. They dipped the huge paint brushes again into the stinking tar. Slap, slap, went the bristles, pounding against Noah's flesh. They reached the softer parts of his body. Sneers and hoots continued.

"Ain't this here something, yellow belly, having your privates painted?" The insults rose up as if from hell.

"Where are the feathers?" Claude Fitzbottom yelled. "Bring on the feathers."

In their hurry they'd forgotten to bring feathers. "Can't have no tar and feathering without feathers," hollered Pudgy Simmons. "Run into the Dutchman's bedroom and bring us out a pillow."

They invaded Sister Nettie's bedroom, grabbing her best goose down pillow. Crash! went the stoneware pitcher, a gift from Nettie's grandmother, shattering on the floor. Then the fear left her. She stood on the porch and prayed for her husband, for her daughters, and for herself. Mercy prevailed, for they did not touch her nor her daughters, who kneeled with frightened faces plastered against the window glass.

Jake Dugan ripped the striped pillow tick with a knife blade long enough to make the devil shudder. "How about feathers? Ain't feathers the right covering for a real Mennonite chicken like you?" The goose feathers descended upon poor Noah, who had not resisted the attack. If he had fought back, he figured he might be already swinging from the maple tree. The feathers covered him. The tar burned his flesh. He could scarcely breathe. The feathers in his mouth choked him. Gagging, he prayed. "Oh Father, give me strength. I pray for these in this hour. Touch them."

Noxious fumes invaded his nostrils and throat, his stomach turned. Burning tar covering his eyes cut off his sight. Struggling, he managed to open his left eye. Noah focused his eye and looked right into the face of the former Mennonite, Benjamin Eicher, tipping back the bourbon bottle.

"Benjamin. Don't you know you were the beloved?" said Noah, tears burning, mixing with the noxious tar at such a callous betrayal. He spoke of Benjamin, the beloved of Jacob, one of the patriarchs in the Bible.

"I was present at your baptism." Benjamin's baptism had not freed him from the slavery of Egypt. He was still in bondage.

Old Tibbon awakened from his blow to the head and saw the stark reality about him. Without even a growl, he leaped forward, sinking his long fangs in Groceryman Happersall's fat buttocks.

"Shoot the yellow belly," Happersall yelled. But the crowd did not comply. They'd had their fun. They'd exhausted themselves. The only thing left to do would be to set fire to the house and let those virgins upstairs come racing out in their nightdresses.

To Noah's dismay, Bodie Spank wheeled around. "Men, ain't you forgetting something important? Ain't took this here man on his ride yet. Hollis, run down there by the pig pen and fetch me a rail!"

"Oh, merciful God," prayed Noah.

The crowd reawakened with new glee.

Two handkerchief-masked, sweating bullies wrenched the rail loose. With wild yells they bounced and carried it along until they stood over Noah's sticky, feathered body. How frail it looked, this farmer's body, naked, mottled with feathers, stinking with gaseous fumes.

Sister Yoder, a wrapper thrown around her, ran forward and held the sticky, precious head of her husband.

Rude shoves sent her sprawling. "Ain't finished with the work. Got to do the final honors. Stay out of the way, else you'll get some tar too," they threatened her.

They dropped the rail recklessly across Noah's body, bruising his loins. He bit his tongue in agony. Splinters scraped his stomach. His ear ached from the piercing knock of the rail against his head.

Silas Woser dragged a bit of rope from his back pockets. "Help me, here, Bodie. Got to tie up the skunk. Ain't an honorable evening without the ride down the lane on this here rail."

They showed him no mercy. Noah's thin body dropped roughly when two ruffians lifted the rail to their shoulders. The ropes cut his wrists and ankles where he'd been tied too tightly. His mouth, plastered up against the rail, filled with splinters. Some teeth jarred loose.

The rail of hewn wood. The cursed tree. Christ had

been nailed upon such a tree. His cross had two beams. But this horizontal beam was enough for a mortal man like Noah Yoder. "Oh, Jesus Christ, my Savior, if you hung upon the rail, upon the hewn wood, how precious is this opportunity to follow your example."

The drunken carriers stumbled and dropped the rail. Noah fainted, and a cloud hid the pearl moon, as if the face of the moon itself refused to look upon such cowards and such brokenness.

The work of the evening finally completed, the vagabond group began to stagger and shove each other down the lane toward their trucks and cars. The night wasn't over. It was time to head for a roadhouse and find some women. That'd put a cap on the evening.

A great silence—akin to the stillness before one worships—hung over Preacher Yoder's little farm.

Never before had Noah felt so surrounded by God. Like Elisha, his spiritual eyes and resources had been fortified through the pain, the humiliation, and the awful taunts. The tar was nothing. The feathers, nothing. The hewn beam providing his carriage only reminded him of his Savior. The insults and taunts—yes, they tore his spirit and rent his soul, humiliating him. But his soul found a footing, like the bottom of a river. Solid rock. All fear vanished.

When Nettie raced to her husband, her tears fell on the black tar and upon his stricken body. She kissed him, smothered him, rocked him. Her weeping rose up, and old Tibbon came over and snuggled against her to comfort her and lick her face.

Sister Yoder set to work scrubbing her husband's body and anointing his assaulted skin. One thing was for certain. When Preacher Yoder rose to stand behind the pulpit the next Sunday, his heart was warmed by new graces and a deep love, even though his hair stood up in thick, stuck-together tufts. His hair, the red burns and splotches from the kerosene and turpentine Nettie had used to remove the tar, and the purple swelling of his broken nose only accented the peace of his gentle face as he prayed: "Let us pray for those who abuse us, for they know not what they do."

Rejoicing and praise rose to God in the plain meetinghouse. They were among those persecuted who knew the meaning of thanks. In the hour of trial, they had experienced the blessed presence of the spirit of Christ.

One day, eighteen months after the war was over and the spasms of the country had subsided, when the fog lifted from the land and from the minds of people bent on harming others, a humbled man came riding onto Noah's farm.

Slouching, the bent man tied his horse to the hitching post and opened the gate leading to the house.

"Noah, that's Walter Happersall," said Nettie in great bewilderment.

Grocer Walter Happersall had not had peaceful nights since the evening of his extreme folly. Somehow he could not get rid of the smell of tar in his nostrils. Even his bourbon bottle didn't satisfy. There had been a perpetual gnawing deep within him, like a rat gnawing at a dank beam.

Noah came out on the porch to greet the sad-faced man.

"Noah Yoder, I have to tell you something." Walter's great dark eyes were ringed with even darker circles. I've slept little since that night we, we ..." Walter could not finish; he broke into sobs.

Noah took the stricken man by the elbow and ushered him into the living room, seating him on the best chair. Nettie walked into the dining room, looking on. What on earth was taking place?

"I have to tell you something, Brother Yoder." What was that, *Brother* Yoder?

"Since I led that dastardly gang of cowards to your place that night ..." Walter again burst into wracking sobs.

Finally, blowing his nose and wiping his bleary eyes, he took hold of himself.

"Brother Yoder, since that awful night, business started going down in my store. A little at first. Then more and more. Goods stacked up. Sales began to slip. Suddenly I had more expenses than profit." He blew his nose again.

"But, Brother Yoder, what I must tell you is that your Mennonite people continued to come to my store. Every day, there were some of your people there, the women in coverings and bonnets, the men, always kind. Even after what I did to you. Will God ever forgive me? Forgive me, Brother Yoder."

"It was what you people call the English, the other people, non-Mennonites, I mean. When they found out what I'd done, they went across the street and bought their groceries from Franklin's Store. God help me, Brother Yoder, the bank foreclosed on my note and I lost the store yesterday. I'm bankrupt."

Chapter 8

It seemed to Barbara that all during the war the weather turned grey and cloudy, dropping mist, cold rain, sickness, and burdens. A dreadful flu broke out, forcing them to stop Sunday services at the meetinghouse. Bishop Hartzler labored through the mud with his team and surrey for seven funerals.

Those who had automobiles left them parked in barns or newly-built garages. Wasn't that something, a building to house an automobile? Extravagance. Change. But who could stop progress? Or was it progress? Didn't seem like it to Barbara. Seemed to her that changes divided people.

Hope—that's what was needed by a Christian in these times. Faith and hope were what counted. God had given Barbara a lot of it through the years. But now, with all this mud, all this fog, that war, those stories, and Seth's letters about all that abuse and ending up in Fort Leavenworth prison—well, to say the least, Barbara's spirits sank a little. When would the war be over, anyway?

Barbara had felt like she had a rock in the pit of her stomach when she got that letter from Seth. Confusion reigned at Camp Funston. Those refusing to wear the uniform or to engage in what President Wilson called noncombatant service were taken care of quickly. Seth was in the military prison at Leavenworth. Chains. Punishment. Torture.

Barbara looked up into the tiny buffet mirror. What should she expect? She supported her family and her church in its precious teachings. She surveyed herself a bit in the mirror. She saw an old woman with hair a cross between white and grey, parted in the middle and pulled back and tied in a knot at the back of her head. Neck wrinkled, too.

Well, Barbara thought, if the sisters of the church would start putting collars on their dresses it would hide some of the crepe look of their necks. But this was no time for finery. She would stick to the old patterns, the plain styles. They were good enough for an old Mennonite woman like herself.

Barbara looked in the mirror again. She saw a woman who had made it this far without being asked to share a bed with a man, and she guessed she'd make it all the way across without one. So what if her sister Salome had blossomed when she got married. Barbara didn't care if they called her an old maid.

It reminded her of when Simon and Seth were little tykes and they wanted to show her how they could swim. They worried her almost to death, so she'd stood on the far edge of the pond, encouraging them and waving to them until they made it all the way across.

That's what life is, isn't it—swimming across? Don't each of us have to paddle across by ourselves? With the help of the Lord, of course. So far Barbara hadn't needed anyone, unlike Salome, except the Lord to help her paddle across this sea of life. Barbara kept warm enough in her bed upstairs at night without a man with pretty eyelashes like Salome had married.

Yes, Barbara was in a slump. Depressed is what you would have to call it. She needed some sunlight, something green like the pawpaw leaves or the wild ferns on the north side of those oaks and cedars on that hillside toward Camp

Branch. So she decided to take a walk in the woods. She didn't need to help Abram Zook with the milking for a couple more hours.

She drew on her overshoes and pulled her raincoat on over her black wool sweater. Grabbing a scarf and wool gloves, she turned the doorknob, and stepped out into the rain.

Her steps took her over the walk of ashes and cinders down past the chicken house and the grainery. She unhooked the gate made of twelve inch boards and walked through. She couldn't forget to hook it. She would be even more depressed if the milk cows got out and she would have to run around in the mud to try to get them back in the lot again.

There it was, up ahead. The woods. Hickory trees stood like solitary sentinels in the damp fog. Mist swirled around the lower branches. Clouds hung over the treetops. The moisture was good for the ground and the growing things. Better than a hard freeze.

Barbara pondered. This was how things were, after all. There was a cycle to life: sunshine, May flowers, green wheat fields and harvest time, then the frost of autumn, nipping everything, giving the growing things notice that it was time to withdraw a bit—time to go into that three-month sleep called winter. Then the cycle started over again.

The sicknesses, this awful war, what had happened to brother Noah that terrible night, the gloomy skies—all of it was a similar kind of withdrawing. What did the apostle Paul say? That in everything God works for good. That means the shadows and dreary times, too, she reminded herself. Even having a nephew in prison. Even Noah's broken nose and getting tarred and feathered. Even the burden the sisters had taken on of coming up with $1,500 a month—that had been Barbara's idea.

The mud felt good beneath her overshoes. With each

step she sank a little, feeling the tug and pull of the mud. She could really burn off some energy on a walk like this. Her coattails dragged through a stand of red-laced buckbrush. Startled, a cottontail rabbit sprang and bounded away.

Suddenly a shaft of golden light pierced the gloom of the fog. The sun, shining above the clouds, had pierced the grey dimness. It reminded Barbara of that pillar of light the Israelites followed.

The sunlight lasted only a minute, but it was enough to remind her that there was a light in the world. She'd done her best to keep her eyes focused on that light of the blessed Lord. Even when she'd gone up to the courthouse to speak to the judge on behalf of her people and what was going on in the community. The menfolk wouldn't have done it. Too forward, they would have said. Might stir up more resentment. Didn't the blessed Jesus give himself over to those who persecuted him?

She had followed her Lord and used the brains he'd given her. She had hooked up Timmon to her buggy and hightailed it over to East Lynne where she parked the buggy and Timmon in the livery stable. Then she had walked right down to the depot and bought herself a round-trip ticket to Harrisonville. She was on her way to see Judge Richer, who had come from one of the old-time Dunker families in the community.

"We want to do something, Judge Richer, to aid the afflicted and needy. Relief contributions. The men of our congregation are bogged down with the farming, the sickness, and all those young men of our community drafted and in prisons or detention camps. Judge Richer, we women can do something. Can we talk about it?"

Barbara sat there in her black stockings and bonnet, waiting for the judge's response. Her eyes, wise as Solomon's, stared right at him. She was not at all nervous.

Dumbfounded, the judge cleared his throat. "Why,

Miss Barbara, I don't know. Your people, you know, have resisted the war. Made a problem in the county. Lot of feeling over it. I don't know." He cleared his throat again.

"You know our beliefs, Judge Richer. This county—with your support—has consistently drafted our young men for detention camps. Some of them are at Leavenworth and Alcatraz, suffering right now. They could be helping with civilian and relief work. President Wilson and the draft boards have kept it all confused. These young men are not being obstinate. They are ready to work, once they are permitted to.

Our community is suffering, Judge Richer. The Klan frightens lonely farm women and children at night. Two of our ministers were taken from their fields and imprisoned in the county jail right here in this very town. For three days they sat there, and they committed no crime at all. I guess you know about my brother, Noah Yoder. He's a minister in our church. We are growing afraid, Judge Richer."

Again, Judge Richer cleared his throat and looked over the top of his wire-framed glasses. Woman's got a lot of guts, he thought to himself. Always did admire a woman with spunk.

Who would have thought an elderly Mennonite woman would have the nerve to come marching in here like that? Judge Richer knew about Barbara's farm. Everybody knew about her place—the huge, red Swiss barn, the famous stonework. Her eleven-room house had been one of the first in the county to install central steam heating.

Those old-fashioned women were workers. Why Lillybelle, his very own wife, showed off those two quilts she'd had Elizabeth Helmuth make for her. One of them surely would have won first prize, had Lillybelle taken it to the state fair.

Unlike those spunky Mennonite women, Judge Richer thought the Mennonite men were quiet. Maybe too quiet.

He knew there had been tar and featherings, and he had almost forgotten about Bishop Ike Hartzler and Preacher Manassah Hershberger who had been thrown in jail. Hadn't he told the sheriff and prosecuting attorney that they didn't have a case? Hadn't he warned them to treat those two men respectfully? You could make life miserable for people, but you couldn't force them to buy war bonds. Maybe this war had caused more craziness and hysteria than he'd accounted for. He'd see what he could do about it.

Those two ministers did have pretty sore wrists from the handcuffs. He'd hated that the sheriff had been so eager to nab them. It happened before he could stop it. He hated that they had nothing to eat but bread and water and had to sleep on the floor without any blankets. They'd had to listen to the hoots and insults of the other jailmates, too. Now this elderly woman was sitting here, smart as one of her peacocks up on her barn roof.

"Tell you what, Miss Barbara," the judge looked at her and smiled, as if he had not known much about the terrors and sufferings of her people. "Tell you what. I believe I can talk to the sheriff and his deputies. I think they'd listen to some reason, especially from me. Wouldn't want the law broken here in Cass County at all."

Barbara could hardly believe what she was hearing. But that widow in the Bible got her wish and desire simply by her "importunity," whatever that was. Maybe this was importunity.

The judge continued. "You women of the Mennonites have that sewing gathering, don't you? Reckon we could arrange with the Red Cross that if you women could raise a good amount each month for relief work, the county'd work along with you. Might put a cushion between you German people and the— uh, the men you talked about."

"What do you call a good amount of money, Judge Richer?" Barbara leaned forward, staring him right in the face with her shiny black eyes, like her mother, Sarah, had.

"How about the sum of, um, how about fifteen hundred dollars a month?"

"A thousand five hundred dollars a month?" Barbara was getting on in years and this blasted her almost out of her chair. Still, she was a survivor. What was money, compared to giving relief to those who suffered, and that included the people right in her church?

"I'll take it up with the sisters. Thank you, Judge Richer. You know, I remember you when you were a little tyke, a little Dunker boy. My mother took pleasure in knowing your mother, back in those hard times."

She did take it up with the sisters. And the sisters listened and agreed. At least, most of them did. So the Mennonite women of the little community gave great sums of money to the Red Cross. The women organized, 300 of them from the two churches. They pledged to raise $1,500 each month for six months. The sisters sold the quilts they made. They baked bread and cakes and pies.

When there was a sale or auction in their group, they provided the lunch. Scrape and toil. Twila and Simon Yoder did what old grandmother Sarah and Aunt Barb and Aunt Salome did so long ago. They hightailed it out to the woods and picked gooseberries. This time they got ten cents a gallon. In the fall, they hurried back, scraping up the walnuts and hickory nuts. Still, pressure breathed down the necks of the people of the little community.

Though they'd agreed, some of the sisters thought that Barbara had been too forward, that she had overstepped the bounds, especially for a woman. Beulah Slagel, after she'd gotten home from sewing, got on her wall phone and rang up Phoebe Bontrager who hadn't been at the sewing.

So Barbara got talked about behind her back. She expected it. She didn't know yet whether or not she'd get a visit from the ministers, the deacon, or even Bishop Ike. But she was prepared for it. She didn't even have to take out that worn piece of paper from her mother's Bible. "There is neither Jew nor Greek, male nor female."

If they came, she'd send them right to their Bibles and let them read about some real women of the Bible–Dorcas, Miriam, Ruth, Priscilla, Esther. That ought to nudge their brains and help them to look at things in a balanced way.

She had reached the edge of the creek, Camp Branch. The water was murky; dead leaves floated on an almost imperceptible current. Even rivers and creeks have their ways. But Barbara knew that in the spring it would flow again with fresh water, and she could sit right here under the new leaves of this giant sycamore and throw in a line and bring home some real nice sun perch and catfish.

Yes, there was a time and season for everything. The walk through the February mist and mud had renewed her. There was a light–within herself–glowing more brightly now. The sun actually had burst through and had moved over toward the west cloud bank. Soon the sky would be dark blue and purple, laced with pink.

She grabbed a broken stick and headed back up that long hill past the pawpaw patch and she began to sing: "Walking in the sunshine, beautiful and bright, In the rosy morning, or the dewy night; Steadily advancing onward day by day, Follow Jesus all the way."

The sun had clouded over again. But she knew there was sunshine in her soul.

Chapter 9

It was May. The lilacs in front of Barbara's house were in full bloom. Swallowtail butterflies hovered in the sweet air. Looking over the little ledge that led down to the lane, one could catch glimpses of foot-high wild roses in clumps of intoxicating pink that smelled sweeter even than the lilacs. Great billows of fleecy clouds swept across the blue sky. A pleasant spring breeze blew—the kind of breeze that kisses the cheek and blesses the heart.

Barbara couldn't believe that Mary Barb had spent a summer at the normal school in Warrensburg, and had already taught two years. And now she was getting married. Ike Miller just better love and appreciate Mary Barb. Barbara wouldn't put up with a slouch of a man marrying her favorite niece. Ike came from good stock. He showed promise on his father's farm. She always had liked Ike's mother, Sadie. Usually sat by her at the quilting. They had lots in common, as her folks also came from Ohio.

Barbara couldn't explain what happened that day Mary Barb told her that she and Ike were getting married. As usual, Mary Barb had come over on Thursday to help with the cleaning.

It wasn't as if she'd been hit cold, right out of the blue. Mary Barb had told her that Ike was writing letters to her. Then one Sunday evening Ike had come walking up the aisle at the meetinghouse with her. Right there on the women's side with the floor slanting upward toward the back of the church.

Ike hadn't stumbled and turned red like some of the other farm boys had done with their Sunday night dates when they came up that aisle and faced the folks gathered there. Ike lifted his head and flashed his gleaming white teeth. Barbara remembered how it had started.

"Alice Schrock and Lydia Bowman and I walked downtown during the noon hour." That was back when Mary Barb was a senior at the high school. "We girls liked to stand in front of the jewelry store and look over the rings and displays in the window. Well, one day Alice Schrock said she'd like to go in and take a better look at those pearl-handled sets. You know—the brush and comb resting on a little oval mirror."

No sooner had she said those words when Mr. Theodore Thompson himself opened the door and invited them in.

"You girls, er— ladies, come on in and look over the things in the store. Get a better look."

They'd gone into Mr. Thompson's store all right, trying not to giggle too much. Mr. Thompson was a bit surprised to see these Mennonite girls with their plain hair and simple dresses standing there looking in his showcase.

"Show you something, ladies?" He called them ladies, because he was a bit stumped. It didn't seem rightly proper to call them girls, as sober and proper as they seemed.

"Oh, no, Mr. Thompson, we're just looking," said Mary Barb. But she would like to have one of those watches that hang on a chain around the neck. Guess it wouldn't do though at her church. The mother-of-pearl comb sets were more than nice. She picked up the brush. It would last a lifetime. But at twenty dollars it was too expensive for her.

"Tell you what, Miss Mary Barb, Miss Alice, Miss

Lydia—I'm going to show you these three sets, one with the pink, one with the blue handles, and one in that soft violet. Why don't you ladies pick out the ones you prefer?"

It would have been bad manners to say, "No, thank you, Mr. Storekeeper, we're just looking," or even worse, "No, Mr. Storekeeper, we're Mennonite girls and our church doesn't hold to worldly things, especially bracelets and rings."

Alice Schrock broke down and started giggling. Lydia Bowman was turning red with such attention focused on her, and since she was taller than the other two, she rocked her heels and stood on her ankles for a moment. Mary Barb started to worry that she'd already stayed downtown too long and would be late for her one o'clock literature class. Then Mary Barb bit.

"Why, Mr. Thompson, let me hold that pink brush. He handed her the brush and the mirror. Mary Barb held the ornate mirror in front of her eyes. Catching a glimpse of her dark hair and her twinkling eyes, she turned, patted the back of her hair, then laughed. "Oh, yes, Mr. Thompson, it's nice, very nice. Can't afford it now. Next year, maybe." Then, to her embarrassment, she broke down and giggled. Oh, if she could only get out of this store.

Teasing, Mr. Thompson told them that before they could get out of the store, they each had to pledge just which of the pearl sets each of them preferred.

Then Mr. Thompson flashed his smile again, as the embarrassed girls finally got enough courage to move on over to the door. Why had their feet stuck to the floor like that? Why were they so dumb?

No sooner had those bashful, plainly combed and dressed girls bent their heads into the west wind, than Mr. Thompson got out the telephone book to look up some numbers and make some calls.

That's when Ike Miller got a call, saying that a very

nice Miss Mary Barbara Yoder had just been in his store and took a great fancy to the mother-of-pearl brush and comb set, and she surely would like it for a present.

Ike wasn't as bashful as most young farmers. Guess he thought it was kind of a privilege to be singled out like that. It sure saved him a lot of time shopping for a Christmas present for his new girlfriend.

"Why, yes. I sold some hogs two weeks ago, Mr. Thompson. Thank you very much. I'll be right over tomorrow when father and I go to the mill. I'll come in your store and pay you for the dresser set. Twenty dollars, did you say?"

When Christmas came and Mary Barb opened the present Ike handed her Sunday evening after church, she nearly fainted. Ike's eyes twinkled and a soft laugh rose from his throat at her reaction. She finally got him to confess that he'd found out from Mr. Thompson that she'd liked the pink dresser set. She nearly fell over on the floor. It took Mary Barb about three years before she forgave Mr. Thompson.

Lydia Bowman's mother made her take her violet-handled set back. It made no difference who gave it to her—it was simply too extravagant. And Alice Schrock's beau, Dollard Swartzentruber, didn't have the twenty dollars to spare, so Alice only got a three-dollar box of handkerchiefs.

That's how it started, the courting and all. The important thing was that Mary Barb was marrying a fine Mennonite man, and if their plans worked out they would soon be moving here, onto Barbara's farm.

Barbara scurried around. She had invited the whole clan over for supper. Afterward, they would take care of some business. They had never settled up the estate after Sarah Yoder died. Salome hadn't needed her share right away, since she married a man who already owned his farm. So Noah said to Barbara, "Take your time. I have all I can handle at the present time on my own farm." But with Ike and Mary Beth getting married, it was time to get things sorted out and make it all legal.

Family, love, service, faith, commitment—all the things her church stood for—all of it would be shared again around her table tonight. Seth, her nephew, was back. Like so many of the young men released from the prison at Fort Leavenworth, he just wasn't the same as before the war. It takes time for wounds to heal; time for all the pain he'd lived through to focus and become clear. One thing she was sure of was that Seth had honored his church and the name of Christ, the prince of peace. She had welcomed Seth home with a tight embrace and a kiss on the cheek.

"By his stripes we are healed." She knew Seth well enough to know that he knew the scars, some still healing on his back, were the wounds of Christ, and that his suffering had been for the profit of his own soul. He needed love, though. Lots of love.

They were so silent, these young men, after they came back from Camp Funston and from the prison. They walked around like those monks she'd run into at that Catholic abbey in St. Joseph—their heads bent down, hands folded, steps slow, and lips silent. It would take time to bring it all together.

Only Simon wouldn't be here tonight. He was off in New York at Union Theological Seminary. Some folks around here didn't take a fancy to that at all. Even the bishop had cleared his throat several times, and sat in silence a long time before he finally coughed out a few words: "Well, a theological seminary has its place." Barbara could tell by the way he said it that there was a lot of uncertainty behind the words. Fear is what it was—fear of change and the influx of the world. It was important not to be conformed to the world.

Simon could have decided differently. He had brains. No one around these parts had even a fourth of the brains of Simon Yoder. But had he overstepped a bit by going to

New York to study? Where would it lead?

White-haired Barbara needed to attend to her potatoes. She planned to boil those new potatoes with the jackets on and serve them with a sprig of freshly cut parsley. She needed to keep her wits about her so she'd be ready to feed twenty-one or so people. She'd try not to think about that small house she'd bought in East Lynne until after the clan left later tonight. Now there was work to do. She still had to make the sauces and the salads and the gravy. She had never served lumpy gravy at her table and she didn't intend to start today.

She stepped out onto the back porch and cut herself a thin slice of gooseberry pie. No, she hadn't lost her touch. She was relieved to find that the bottom crust was done. Who wanted to sit at her table and eat pie with unbaked dough on the bottom?

Then she chuckled as she heard her tractor, the big lug-wheeled Chase that Abram Zook, the hired man, was driving around the bend by the pond and on over toward the shed. She had to keep up with the times. She'd sell the tractor to Ike and Mary Barb, too. Wouldn't want them starting out in farming without the proper equipment.

Her laughter rose up, mingling with the outside breeze beyond the morning glories stretching up on her porch.

Chapter 10

The day Barbara first got the tractor she stood and stared in wonder as Abram plowed, watching the furrows turn over like water in front of a ship on the sea. Then she got bold. When Abram made a turn in front of her at the end of the furrow, she told him to get off the tractor.

Barbara, without her sunbonnet, climbed up on that monster made of iron and still smelling like new paint. Fumes from its exhaust pipe floated over her head.

"How do I get it going?"

Abram was frightened, but he was smart enough not to lock horns with the one who paid him. Besides, he knew his boss had fortitude and guts, and he couldn't remember when Barbara didn't succeed at whatever she laid her hands upon.

"You've got to put your foot on that pedal and let it out."

Well, Barbara put her heel on that pedal and let it out with a mighty lurch. A flock of blackbirds in the hedge rose up in fright. Smoke rose in ascending puffs from the exhaust pipe, like those smoke messages the Indians send from the hilltops. Barbara, clutching the iron wheel in nervous glee, hunched her back and lurched ahead.

Oh, how good it felt. Here she was, *modern,* keeping up with the times. The lurching and jerking of that iron tractor, and the heaving of her foot on that pedal made her feel like a young girl again.

Let others sit on the sulky plow; she was sold on the tractor. She remembered the tug of the team when she followed behind the walking plow—don't try to tell her about jerks. That jerked your guts right out onto the prairie sod.

Abram was put out. He had to sit under the shade of the Osage orange hedge until she'd plowed almost half an acre. When Barbara climbed down, her face was wreathed in the biggest smile Abram had ever seen. Working for Miss Barbara had its fun points. He knew her well enough to figure that after wheat harvest, when he would paint that big Swiss barn, she'd probably tell him to get down from the ladder and let her do the pointed eaves forty feet above the ground.

Then too, she allowed that when the family gathering was over, she wanted him to take her up to the county seat where she planned to conk down $800 and bring home one of those Model T Fords.

Abram didn't know why women like Barbara needed to wear coverings on their heads. Men around here dipped their heads in respect to her. Even the bishop and the ministers cleared their throats and stepped back a little when she came over from the women's side with her Bible open, checking up on a point mentioned in the morning sermon.

He remembered that time she'd been so forward as to hightail it all the way up to the county seat and talk to the judge about this war stuff—the Liberty Bonds, the tarring and featherings—and win him over to let the Mennonite women do service through the Red Cross and relief agencies. There had been some talk about setting her back at communion time. But it passed, since it worked out for the good of everyone.

Mary Barb drove down the lane in her father's 1925 Chevrolet touring car and parked right in front of the buggy stile. She raced up the steps and yelled for her aunt.

"Auntie Barb, Auntie Barb!" Mary Barb cried out.

In spite of the rheumatism in her left knee, Barbara jumped up, nearly spilling the pan of apples she was peeling for pies. The screen door jerked open and Barbara saw Mary Barb's face, flushed hot pink. Her hair swept around her forehead, not pinned back tight like a proper girl ought to do her hair.

"I'm getting married. Ike Miller asked me to marry him. Auntie Barb, isn't it wonderful?" Mary Barb blurted and Barbara could see she was blooming with joy.

Her message hit Barbara like a bolt out of the blue. It felt as if someone had pulled a thick wall down between her and the world, and that included Mary Barb, too. Barbara tried to smile. But she didn't kiss her niece, instead she patted her on the shoulder.

"Calm down, Mary Barb, your father wouldn't approve of such excitement." Barbara's words sounded scratchy, like rusted tin. A grey pall engulfed her mind and soul, like fog covering the land.

Barbara took up her pan of apples again without even inviting Mary Barb to grab a pan and a knife to help her.

Thank God, Mary Barb understood and took it well. The wall between them stood all day. Suddenly nothing seemed worthwhile. None of her efforts, or her life itself. Worse yet, she had to take out her handkerchief from her apron pocket and blow her nose, raise her glasses, and wipe an eye. Awful morning it was.

Mary Barb calmed herself down. Aunt Barb mattered to her. She knew that Barbara felt cut off and left out. She had seen it when Aunt Salome surprised them all and married Mose Lehman. Marriage had sure been good for Aunt Salome, though. Now she even wore one of those new style coverings at church.

Barbara jumped up to check her potatoes. Her knee gave her a sharp pain. She made a mental note to send off for that remedy mentioned in the *Capper's Weekly*. She doubted her life that day. Loneliness overshadowed her. Suddenly her farm didn't seem worthwhile or friendly. It felt more like a place for the lonely wind blowing down the lane, the flowers all faded. Just dust and dry grass, and the wind howling through the knotholes in the barn.

Even her peacocks seemed a great bother to keep just for their beauty. Then, too, her church didn't seem to appreciate beautiful things. She'd like to have taken a big bouquet of her peonies to church last spring, but she knew that it wouldn't go over. Folks said she'd been forward and acting just like her mother when she bothered that judge. That was not woman's work, that was definitely work for a man, she'd been told.

The whole day she couldn't think of anything to say to Mary Barb. She tried. But it seemed fake and forced. Every word between them felt like trying to bend rusty fence wire. Then Barbara remembered what Jeremiah in the Bible had said: "He hath turned aside my ways, and pulled me in pieces: he hath made me desolate."

Then the worst happened. On Counsel Sunday, the holy day of preparation for communion a week later, she'd been blamed for working on the Sabbath. Even worse, that snoopy Phoebe Bontrager had accused her. And to think, she'd rented Widow Phoebe that four-room house on the south edge of her east forty acres for practically nothing.

Later she found out Phoebe's husband Milo had left her with two ten-gallon cream cans filled with greenbacks of sizable denominations. He hadn't believed in banks. Instead, he banked it in the earth—land owned by Barbara herself. Phoebe had run to the bishop and told him that it was pitiful, but did he know that Barbara Yoder, who lived off the main road in the woods, worked on Sunday?

The meeting had gone like usual. Sacred hush. Holy songs. Meetinghouse packed. One could feel the blessed healing balm of Christ among the believers: staid, dressed in plain grey, brown and blue, black, too. Search closely over their clothing; they kept to regulations. Only Lila Zehr had to take off the white collar she'd put on over her navy dress before she came back next week for communion. That was a small matter. But desecrating the Sabbath was something else.

Barbara still tasted gall when she thought of it. Bitter gall. And Sister Phoebe, well, Barbara Yoder had to pray a lot, on her knees too, in the upstairs closet. Never prayed in the south bedroom closet upstairs before. This was a matter that needed special grace and special forgiveness. Had to find a secret place and pray over the boiling gall that had arisen.

They'd sung that blessed hymn: "O Lamb of God, still keep me near to thy wounded side; 'Tis only there in safety And peace I can abide. What foes and snares surround me, What doubts and fears within! Thy grace that sought and found me alone can keep me clean."

Barbara sat there. The blessed atmosphere bathed her. She examined her soul, too, making sure that she was prepared to return and take of the cup and the bread the following Sunday.

Then Bishop Hartzler asked that searching question: "Is there any matter between you? Is there one who, before bringing your gifts to the altar, has a charge against you?"

Nobody ever remembered a woman rising on Counsel Sunday. So it shocked the congregation when Phoebe Bontrager stood up. Her long neck rose up like a cabbage stalk with her scraggly hair and thin face wobbling atop it. She swept back a covering string, cleared her throat and said, "Sister Barbara Yoder and her hired man, Abram Zook, desecrated the Sabbath, June 17th, 1924."

No one could recall such a silence as the one that followed in the meetinghouse. Surely the angels above were holding conversation with one another over this.

Barbara froze. What was Phoebe talking about?

"You need to be specific, Sister Bontrager," the bishop

said. He looked wan and worried at this "monkey wrench" that had gouged the peaceful atmosphere of such a holy day.

"Bishop Hartzler, I'm sorry to have to say this. But Sister Barbara Yoder and her hired man, Abram Zook, were working on Sunday. I heard a cattle truck come down her lane on Sunday night, June 17th. I couldn't sleep on account of the coyotes over there in Barbara's ditch keeping me awake. While I was up I heard them loading cattle. I finally took some Aspirin and looked at my clock before I went back to the bedroom. That cattle truck drove out of her lane at exactly eleven fifty three. It was still Sunday night, Bishop Hartzler. Not Monday morning."

Then Sister Phoebe sat down. She drew her face together as peacefully as she could, her pious work accomplished.

Jolted off his guard, the bishop cleared his throat, and turned to the three black-clothed ordained men sitting behind him on the bench. They rose and the four of them circled for a whispered conversation.

Barbara was smart enough not to rise to her feet and defend herself. She followed the defenseless Jesus, her master. It might take six months to straighten this out, so she'd have to bypass communion this time. She wasn't about to stand up and counter Sister Bontrager in the meetinghouse, packed like it was that day.

The bishop and ministers met with Barbara afterwards in the little anteroom on the east side of the church. Barbara kept her dignity. Didn't everybody know what a slouch Phoebe was? Chances were that she forgot to wind her clock anyway. Besides, Barbara remembered when Phoebe bought that clock at the used furniture store. She only paid a dollar for it. According to Barbara's clock, Heavener Styles drove that truck into her barnyard at exactly eleven minutes after one on Monday morning, June 18th.

Barbara had to suffer the doubting glances of the

brothers and the sisters of the meetinghouse that day. But she kept quiet. She knew the truth in her heart. Heavener, the truck driver, was good testimony. She could think of at least a dozen Mennonite men who called Heavener when they had cattle or hogs to be shipped up to Kansas City.

She left the meetinghouse and hurried to her buggy. She gave a real hard slap on old Timmon's rump as they made dust getting home. Barbara hated not getting this situation untangled for six months; she couldn't partake of the holy emblems of communion until that fall. She understood why Jeremiah wrote the verse in Lamentations: "I was a derision to all my people."

No one ever knew for certain whose clock was wrong, Barbara's or Phoebe's.

Chapter 11

Barbara watched Noah and Nettie walk up the sidewalk toward the north porch. She took pride in Noah and what he'd done in the church. He preached well and the young folks liked him. They sat still and listened. Noah had shortened his sermons, and used good illustrations. To Barbara's knowledge, those benches up front where Seth once carved his name stayed repaired. Some credit for that surely went to the ministers.

Yes, ministers of the church had weights on their backs. She knew Noah's concern about the church and the blessed young people. Separation from the world was important for Noah.

Look at the times. It seemed like the floodgates had opened. One day women had their skirts at least down to their shoe tops. Next day they split the breeze with flapper dresses at mid-thigh. Barbara thought it was just terrible.

She likened it to that new book by F. Scott Fitzgerald, *This Side of Paradise*. It certainly didn't take a fool to find out that we still live this side of heaven. Maybe wars always broke things open, whipping up the winds of loneliness.

Barbara knew she was getting older, but when she saw those girls with bobbed hair on the square at Harrisonville smoking cigarettes, she nearly fell over. They had their stockings rolled too, down low on their calves. No wonder the ministers worried.

She'd seen pictures of what the well-dressed young gentleman wore too: sailor straw hats, bell-bottom trousers that fit too tightly, with a pocket for a hip flask.

Prohibition hadn't stopped folks from swilling spirits. She'd gotten wind that the rich folks up at the county seat held wild parties and made gin in a bathtub.

Barbara respected the way her sister-in-law, Nettie, dressed. She wore a black bonnet on her head—the old style, tied under her chin. Her white silk covering strings fell down over her shoulders. Cape on her dress. Simple black shoes and black stockings anchored her dress—the hem down where it did some good—to the ground.

And the spending? Folks went wild, even some of the Mennonites. They bought and sold. Tore down fences and expanded their farms. Banks had lots of money to lend and made it easy to buy another hundred acres. Low interest rates at the bank—only 4 or 5 percent, meant there was no way a fellow could lose. Weather cooperated, too. Rains came aplenty, everything burst out green all over.

Seth and Sonya and their toddler, Timothy, drove in. Seth parked under the blooming locust tree. The intoxicating sweetness of the drooping white blossoms filled the air. Seth was doing well. Plowing the land gave him time to ponder what had happened to him. And no one could better soothe a troubled soul or brow than Sonya.

How young they looked. Sonya had braided her gold hair and wound it around her shining face. Seth, broad shouldered like his father, had dark eyes that focused straight on you when he talked. They kept to the plain ways. He didn't even wear a tie.

Barbara had just seated her company in the living room when she heard the purring of Mose Lehman's Oldsmobile, the one with the flashy headlights and the spare tire on the running board. She looked out the window and saw Salome seated beside Mose. She had gained weight, but who wouldn't, eating the rich food like they did up on his farm. Barbara would never have split the air through this community like Salome did without her bonnet on her head. Barbara hoped Mose would keep to himself when it came time to settle up the legal work.

The back door of Mose's Oldsmobile opened and out sprang Twili, who had just gotten back from Ohio. Barbara smiled and ran outside to greet her niece. She was glad to have Twili join the family again. Twili had decided more than a year ago to go to school in Ohio with Cousin Samantha. Barbara wondered what new ideas Twili might have brought back with her.

At supper, Twili stunned Barbara when she asked, point-blank: "Aunt Barb, did you ever date anyone?"

That's what the matter was these days, Barbara thought, girls acted too forward. She couldn't really think how to answer Twili's question. Blushing, Barbara's work-worn hand brushed aside a few wisps of snow-white hair. "Why Twili Yoder, such a question. Such a question."

She wouldn't let that question buffalo her. She'd wade on through, then change the subject quickly as she could.

"As a matter of fact, Menno Bender used to take me to evening services when I was a little younger than you." Now why did she have to say it like that? Anyway, she continued. "Menno liked to take me to services. Always thought that we sang so well together."

Menno had liked her a lot. But then she came down with the scarlet fever and had to stay home all that spring. When summer came and she did get back to Sunday evening services, there sat Menno with Berta Roth. No, Barbara couldn't say she never had a date. Things the way they were in this community back in those days, though, fellow started to date a girl more than two times on Sunday evening found himself on a track that usually led to the bishop's house for a marriage ceremony.

She hadn't gotten past the second date. Sometimes she still pondered it. How would her life have been different if she'd married Menno? Would she be living way out west in Idaho where he and Berta settled? Would Barbara's love for her family and for Missouri have kept him here? She wondered how they were, Berta and Menno. She and the girls had talked about taking the train out to Idaho to see cousins. Most likely they would run into Menno and Berta there, too.

She had gotten through that one quite well. What would that brazen niece ask her next? Still, she was glad to have Twili home. If Twili behaved herself Barbara might ask her to take that trip with her out west. There was something about Twili; she and Barbara were alike in many ways. Neither of them took things too seriously. They could be serious, mind you, but they weren't worriers or face-down-to-the-earth ponderers, like Noah and Seth. Both she and Twili liked to throw back their heads and laugh a little.

Barbara sawed at her smothered steak. My, she thought, can't keep eating beef with my teeth like this. Getting older was kind of like a barn falling apart—a hinge loose here, hole in the roof there. Repairs. Repairs. She'd repaired her teeth, regular as most sisters of the church.

Mose Lehman, who liked to be the authority, told her she ought to get her some of those new store-bought teeth. His mother, Priscilla, had a pair. Hadn't she noticed?

Barbara had noticed. She thought they looked nice, that they made her look at least ten years younger. But they looked a mite big for Priscilla's mouth. Some folks said they made her look horsy.

Priscilla said all you had to do to clean them was to pitch them in a glass of water at night and throw in two little pellets that fizzed the water all up. Wonderful, these new things. She'd have to get down to the dentist at Garden

City next week and ask about new store teeth. Especially before they took that trip out west.

After supper they decided to take their chairs out under the cedar trees in the west end of the yard to catch the cool evening breeze. They would talk out there while evening settled. How pretty the pond looked, reflecting the sunset like a mirror. Cattails rose up, lush and green, on the south side. Frogs encouraged them to stick to the task at hand. "Don't give up, don't give up," they croaked.

"I had lawyer Detweiler draw up all these papers," began Barbara. Now that she had started letting go of this place she'd managed all these years, it didn't seem so easy. But, there was a time and season for everything. "Don't hog a whole farm and an eleven-room house just for yourself, Barbara Yoder," she told herself nightly lately, as she struggled with all the legal papers.

"Noah, the southeast 120 acres is deeded over to you. That includes the rental house where Phoebe Bontrager lives." Barbara coughed a little, getting that name out. "Good land. You know I had the portion down there by Clearfork tiled. Rich land that will bring in nice income when farmed properly."

Why did this seem so difficult? She felt ropes tugging at her insides, pulling her. Wasn't this her land? Her bones and muscles had plowed it, her eyes and heart overseeing it through thick and thin? She remembered the onslaught of the plague of grasshoppers, back in 1875. Of course, Noah swept up grasshoppers, too. He had helped save the farm by picking gooseberries and blacking his hands shelling those walnuts.

"Salome, we've talked about this. You said that since you married," Barbara wanted to say, "married well," but held her tongue, "you didn't need land. You'd take your share in cash. Here it is. One hundred twenty acres, same as Noah, cash value at seventy dollars an acre, agreed upon by your husband, Mose, as a fair price. Let's see, that's $8,400." Barbara stretched out her brown, calloused fingers and handed her the check.

"Now, Mary Barb and Ike. This land's a sacred place to me. I'm renting the remaining 160 sixty acres to you. Ike, you'll owe me one third of the earnings from the cash crops. That's according to custom in this community. Buildings, house, barn and all, go with it. If you pay for any repairs, save the bill for me, and I will deduct it from your portion. If I need to repair or paint something, it's your responsibility to let me know."

There, she'd said it. She didn't feel so bad after all. She didn't even cry. Besides, she'd gone over to East Lynne last week and walked through that five-room house and allowed that, yes, she could live there just fine.

And, she could finally stop putting off buying herself that car. Next week she was going to the Ford dealer and plunking down her $800. She could drive a tractor. A car would be nothing compared to that.

Barbara could tell that the arrangements more than satisfied everyone. The evening had gone smoothly, but then, they had always worked together well. They learned that way back when they were children under the arm of her father, Solomon, and her mother, Sarah. They couldn't have settled this country without families sticking together.

Before they scattered for the night, Barbara read them the long letter she'd received last week from Simon. Marvelous how Simon was doing. He had decided to apply for the position of president at that Mennonite college in Indiana.

Nettie and Noah received letters from Simon, too, but he always poured out his deepest feelings and thoughts to his Aunt Barbara.

Barbara hurried over the preliminaries in the letter, getting to the part that had moved her the most: *Auntie Barb, I must tell you how I felt when I left that Sunday morning on the train from Missouri. When I thought of all of you at the meetinghouse down in that little vale, hovering under the arching sycamores, my heart ached to be with you. I sang to myself the hymn I thought you might be singing: "To thy temple I repair; Lord, I love to worship there, When within the veil I meet Christ before the mercy seat."*

"We sing it, yes, we do," said Ike Miller, smiling through his white teeth. "It does have beautiful harmony."

"Well," said Noah, "Words aren't enough to tell you how I'd like to have Simon here when we gather for worship. He is right. That hour is sacred and holy. Simon always knew Christ was present."

Noah took out a red handkerchief and wiped a tear.

"But, God called him for a special work. I don't understand it all. Simon knows it takes faithful communities to bring up faithful servants," said Barbara, picking a lightning bug off her sleeve.

Then she continued from the unfolded pages. *You feel it too, Aunt Barb—the holy hush of the assembled worshipers, waiting for God to touch us, the renewal, the marvelous harmony of those songs offered up from our souls.*

"Yes," said Nettie, listening to each word. "Simon used to tell me he just couldn't think of those who'd fallen away from our church, how he couldn't even imagine how they can exchange pleasures of the world for the bliss and the touch of God in those hours of worship. He used to say, 'What do they do on Sunday morning, Mother? Aren't they torn apart? How can they bear the pain?' Well, I know what Simon would do. He would drop everything to join in singing those words, 'Lord, I love to worship there.'"

Noah cleared his throat. How lovely was the evening and the smell of the cedar.

Barbara read some more: *Change will come, Auntie Barb. There will be ache in the hearts of those who find it difficult, but it will come. You can see it already. I believe that the great emphasis that our bishops have placed upon our people being a "separate" people and also the regulations of dress, order, ways of doing things that have set us apart are very much like a religious community among the Catholics. Our emphasis upon prayer and the holy life, separate unto God, is similar to what one finds in those communities. Monks and sisters take vows. We take our baptismal vows with great seriousness.*

Twili decided to chip in a few words. "Do you think the time will come when we no longer wear plain clothes? Simon used to tell me that emphasizing them and our coverings likened us to a Catholic religious group. Do you think so?"

"Those things must be freely chosen. They lose their meaning if they are done because of heavy-handed ministers or bishops," added Noah, again. His pensive eye caught the willow fronds floating at the edge of the pond.

"They do help us build a sense of togetherness, a sense of community. But they are no substitute for honest, upright living," added Nettie. She approved of plain clothes. Wore them herself.

"I think Simon is right. Listen to this," Barbara added: *In the years ahead, Auntie Barb, we will see great changes. These cultural marks will pass. In the not too distant future, I believe some community of our faith will select a devout sister for the ministry. You always told us about Grandmother Sarah Yoder, her strength, her faith, and her favorite verse: "There is neither Jew nor Greek, male nor female."*

When Barbara took off her glasses and stopped reading at that portion about the possibility of some Mennonite community ordaining a sister of the congregation, Noah's face drew down. He held his right elbow in the palm of his left hand and tilted his face upward.

Pondering, he remembered his mother quoting those words. Did he really believe them? And Nettie, peaceful, quiet and loving Nettie—the sister in the congregation who never had a critical word for anybody. A woman of prayer and kindness. No one could argue about the grace that filled this woman's heart and soul.

Her plainly parted hair and beautiful prayer covering accented her spirit. Her plain, cape dress—a regulation garb, like a regulation garb of a sister in a convent—set her apart. It signified the commitment she had made. These earthly symbols pointed to holy and eternal truth: that the Christian is separate from the world in mind, spirit, and body.

Barbara skipped over the paragraph about how Simon's parents—set apart, plain and orderly, like that monk and sister he'd written about—might have a very difficult time with his letter. *Still,* he wrote, *Isn't it wonderful how people deal with change? Grace and love, once experienced, lift the soul above contradiction, above controversy and quarreling.*

Nothing in this world is permanent, all changes, all is finite. Only the grace and love of God endure from generation to generation. Faith and grace—gifts from God—not human vision or strength enable the soul to face the future and the changes that come with it.

She finished reading. God had been with them that evening. Glittering stars twinkled, spreading out from the great swirl of the Milky Way. The pearl moon had risen over the tall stand of hickory and oaks, eastward, past the orchard. The frogs in the pond now chorused together, "Better have hope, better have hope."

Simon's letter stirred his family's minds and souls. That's the blessing of having a thinker like Simon in the family. He challenged them to the seriousness of this life, and to the meaning of religion.

They parted, reflecting on how Aunt Barbara had

taken the dividing up of the farm and signing over the rental agreements to Mary Barb and Ike. "God bless her," they prayed. "God bless Aunt Barb. Continue to fill her with courage for her future."

Barbara had that pioneer spirit of Solomon and Sarah. Her life of hard work, her bending back and calloused hands all gave testimony, highlighted by the grace and touch of God on her kindly face—wrinkled, yes—and within her eyes, so filled with love.

When Barbara finally lay down upon her bed that night in the southwest bedroom upstairs, a feeling of relief swept over her. She'd taken to sleeping here on account of the large windows, west and south. She could see the great full moon, the sweep of the evening clouds, the starry night. The room stayed light most of the night. It felt warmer, too. In this room with the window open she could go to sleep, lulled by the eerie call of the whippoorwills down on Clearfork Creek.

Chapter 12

Ike and Mary Barb named their first child, Nancy Barb, after her great-aunt, Nancy Yoder, who died tragically in the Border Wars so long ago. Her middle name came from her mother, Mary Barb, and her great-aunt, Barbara Yoder, who lived in the little green house in East Lynne.

The spirit of her namesake overshadowed the child. She did not have her mother's dark hair and eyes. The shining blue eyes beneath the golden hair bore an uncanny resemblance to the eyes of her long dead great-aunt.

Nancy Barb was a gentle child. Neither parent could remember her being cross or when she last cried. She blossomed with joy at the birth of her brother David. She would have none of the pouting jealousy that so often comes to the surface when a child sees a baby brother or sister for the first time.

Joy alone seemed to rule her heart. When Mary Barb held her on her lap and read her stories about Jesus and his mother, Nancy Barb's face didn't reflect a look of enchantment. Rather, the change in her countenance reflected a spiritual knowing.

Some children seem born to goodness. Some children sense the right thing to do, because their hearts are near heaven and still full of grace and forgiveness and love.

Like the Nancy who had lain sleeping for nearly sixty

years beneath the whispering pines, this child wanted to learn. She wanted to read by herself, and to sing the songs her mother and father sang at the meetinghouse.

When she leafed through the old leather-bound book, *Martyrs Mirror,* tears ran down her cheeks as she surveyed the engravings of the people of her faith being drowned or burned at the stake.

Though only five years old, Nancy took care of her fat little brother, Dave, as if he were the Christ child. She adored him as he waddled and toddled after her.

Out in the field her father shook and bounced on the new Farmall tractor. He could plow at least one third again as much with this new monster that crawled across the field with its wheels of spade lugs.

He'd traded off that old Chase of Aunt Barbara's. He still owed her $400 on it, but he'd get that paid off come fall when the wheat and corn came in. Ike had been more than challenged by these 160 acres. He hadn't figured that farming for himself would be such demanding work. In a year or two, he planned to get rid of most of the milk cows. That's what he'd do. Specialize and rent more land to plow. Focus in one direction.

Turning the heavy machine at the end of the furrow, he put it in neutral and sat awhile under the shade of a giant elm tree. He reached up with one brown hand and removed his straw hat. With the other hand he pulled out his red handkerchief and wiped away the heavy beads of sweat that ran down his forehead.

His mind wandered as he thought about how prosperous life had been since the war. Didn't rightly know how President Hoover in Washington could pull it all together, but folks around here kept breaking sod in new fields, buying more mules or tractors, building bigger barns, increasing their milk or stock cattle herds. It took him awhile to get used to the new ways in town, too. Oh, the way people were spending money. People even bought fresh baked bread in town instead of baking it themselves.

He smiled, glad that Mary Barb still insisted on serving her own homebaked bread and rolls. But he sure wished she'd let up on comments like, "Hadn't we better slow down a bit," and "Don't you think that is too expensive," and "Maybe we ought to pay dear old Auntie Barb for her tractor before we swap for a new one."

As far as Ike was concerned, the sky was the limit. Look at the weather. Rains came in the spring and cool early summer. The wheat had no rust in it. No late summer rains ruined the oats or wheat in the field. When it did rain it came down steady and gentle. The seasons flowed like they ought to. He'd heard his folks tell of dry spells, three years or so with hardly any rain at all. He guessed those days were long past.

Ike placed his foot on the clutch, released the hand brake, opened the throttle, and eased the mammoth tractor to the west to begin opening up new furrows.

Over in East Lynne, Barbara put the last pins in her bun at the back of her head, grabbed her bonnet and brought it over the back of her head, then forward. She slid in a big hat pin through the back. Barbara kept up with the times—only the old women of the church still tied their bonnets under their chins. She had cut the strings off. It just felt better this way. Besides she wasn't quite seventy yet—certainly not old enough to be set in her ways.

Sometimes she actually wondered why she'd given up her farm. She wouldn't mind going out there herself and trying out that new tractor Ike had brought home. Though she couldn't help wondering what was the matter with her old tractor, the Chase. Wasn't it about time Ike finished paying her for that one? But these thoughts passed, scattered like the wind blowing through a thistle and spreading the down over the countryside.

Today was Barbara's day and she was not going to let anybody spoil it. A broad smile spread over her face as her feet hit the front porch. Arthur Hostetler was here to take her up to Harrisonville. She had her checkbook with her and over $12,000 in the bank over on Main Street. Thank the Lord. She had more than enough to keep her until St. Peter called her home.

She strode on down to Arthur's car, which vibrated and shook in time to the rattling motor. She climbed in alongside him. Clutching her leather purse in her lap, she looked over to Arthur's tanned face. "This here lady's gonna get her a car today, Arthur. Let's get goin'! Hightail it out of here!"

It took them about a half-hour to reach Harrisonville. She could have taken the train, but riding like this with Arthur in his Plymouth, she could observe just how he did it, this driving. After all, there was not much to it: Keep on your side of the road. Give it gas. Step on the brake now and then. If anyone gets in your way, blast the horn. The only thing that worried her a little was letting out the clutch so it wouldn't jerk your bonnet off.

"No, thank you, Arthur, I won't need a ride home." No words sounded so special, so truthful, so welling up from within one's heart as those words. Barbara meant it.

The car salesman was more than glad to greet a new customer. Mr. Boyd Dorrance himself, owner of the franchise, stepped forward to greet this elderly Mennonite woman.

"Interested in buying a car, Mrs., Mrs., —"

What on earth was an older Mennonite woman doing here all alone, black bonnet on her head, too?

"Barbara Yoder, Miss Barbara Yoder's the name."

Barbara dipped her bonnet a little, still smiling. Felt like she did that time when she ate Crackerjacks for the first time.

"More'n pleased to meet you, Miss Barbara Yoder. Come to think of it, I've heard of you. Aren't you the

Barbara Yoder who lives over east on that farm, the one with the big Swiss barn?"

Well, cut the preliminaries. Barbara wasn't interested in passing the time of day, no, thank you. She had her eyes on that shiny Ford sitting there, gleaming like a black snake that had just crawled out of the woods showing off its new skin. Barbara walked over to it, put her hands on the thin, tin door and peered inside, glancing at the wooden wheel. Wood under your hands would feel good, she thought.

"You like to sit in that Ford, Miss Yoder?"

My, how nice Mr. Dorrance was. She had heard that these men who sold cars were especially friendly and nice.

"Don't mind at all if I do." He opened the door and Barbara lifted her leg—same as lifting it for the buggy step, only this time not quite so high. My, how those imitation leather seats loomed up. She settled herself. Black too, matched her stockings and bonnet. Plain, like their church over there. But wouldn't a body get dizzy, sitting way up high like this, peering out without any reins in your hands. Just that little bump of a motor out in front. What kept it from falling off, anyway? My goodness, didn't it give you a scare without the rump of a horse or two to steady things out and give it balance up ahead? Sitting way up like this, grabbing that wheel made her think she was on the edge of a big hole.

The dizzy spell passed and Barbara climbed out. That was the way with all new things. Remember the big, wood alcohol powered steam iron she'd ordered? When it finally arrived and she got the alcohol poured in the little tank and pumped it up with the little screw of a pump on the handle, lit a match, turned the valve and got ready to do a full day's ironing, what did the sorry thing do but let out a hiss, then "whoop!" it all flamed up around her hand.

Had to turn it off and wait until it cooled before she could try it again. Well, she did hope she'd have better luck with her Ford than that iron, because she never did get the hang of it. The next time it blew up in her face like that she took two steps over toward the back porch and gave that iron a mighty heave out into the garden. She never told anyone about it either, although Phoebe Swartzentruber kept bragging about how nice it was to iron with her new wood alcohol powered steam iron.

"And, may I ask, how much is this Ford, Mr. Dorrance?"

If she was to keep up, she had to go all the way. This car would fit right into the stall in the horse and buggy barn at the meetinghouse. Wouldn't have to worry about old Timmon getting cold out there on communion day when the service was so long.

"Why, Miss Yoder, give you a real deal on that Ford. Eleven hundred dollars. Wouldn't do that for just anyone, but I know you folks take pity on the homeless and I know what you done for the Red Cross awhile back."

Barbara about fell out of her high perch up there on that puckered seat. "Eleven hundred dollars? My, things must have gone up, Mr. Dorrance. I've been holding onto my money for a car, but I hadn't planned on letting go of that much." She pondered.

She opened and closed the thin door. My, how tinny it sounded. She worried that if she tipped this thing over on the frozen ruts in the winter roads it might break apart. Well, she had come here to buy a car. She could understand how things went up after the war.

She guessed she could keep on with her buggy and horse, but it sure did take a lot of time to get to services that way. Besides, with a car like this she could pop over to see how Mary Barb was doing there in her old farmhouse, and sit down and tell stories to chubby little Dave and little Nancy Barb who loved the Lord so much.

Looking around, Barbara's eye spotted a larger, shiny,

heavy looking car. Whatever kind of Ford this was, it was more like what she had in mind. She hadn't expected the Fords to be so thin and tinny. Climbing down, she asked, "Mr. Dorrance, how much is that Ford over there?"

"Why, Miss Barbara, that isn't a Ford. That's a year-old car, good as new. Ferris Hollinger, the banker, traded it in for a new Ford for his wife and he bought himself a new Buick. The car you have your eyes on is a Buick."

"A Buick?" Well, sitting there stretched out, shining, long, a real hood that surely covered more than a bump like the Ford, it certainly had its finer points. "Mind if I take a look, Mr. Dorrance."

Of course Mr. Dorrance didn't mind. He could smell the money, and this old Mennonite woman was surely tired of throwing a blanket over her horse in the winter, tired of getting out in the cold and frost and hooking up the crop strap under the tail. Nope. He didn't blame her at all.

A big smile spread over Barbara's wrinkled face as she ran her hand over the gleaming finish of the Buick's high, sturdy fender. It spread out long and handsome with a trunk on the back and a spare tire mounted gracefully behind the trunk. It was a real wonder.

Then she noticed the heavy running board with the tool chest and the nickel-plated foot steps, and even space for a spare bucket of gas, and water and oil cans. She could take this car on that trip out west. Yes, this was more like what she had in mind. Her liver still shook from the vibrations of Arthur's Plymouth. She didn't want to bring home anything like that.

"Miss Yoder, that's a Buick Touring Car, seven passenger. You could take all your friends there in East Lynne to church in that car." He was right—it did bother her, those widows and single folks with no regular way to get out to the meetinghouse. She could load them up and serve the Lord with this car, for sure.

By this time Barbara had actually lifted herself up into the driver's seat of the magnificent car. That part of her that'd loved peacocks and their brilliant tails and graceful forms took over.

"Why, Mr. Dorrance, this here's real leather I'm sitting on, isn't it?" Her smile spread wider as she grasped the mahogany wheel and looked ahead to where the car's shiny, heavy bonnet covered the giant motor out front. This was more like it. Sitting here she didn't feel like she was on the edge of a cliff. She aimed her eye straight out over the gleaming winged hood ornament, balanced by the perfectly formed headlights rising up. Barbara could feel in command in this car, behind this wheel.

"Car's got overdrive, a clock, turn signals, and wind wings," continued Mr. Dorrance. He leaned in toward the old woman with the smile of a schoolgirl who'd just turned down everyone in the ciphering match. The smell of his shaving lotion rose up to her flaring nostrils. A nice man, she thought, knows a lot, too. What on earth were all those parts of this car that he'd mentioned?

"It's got a vacuum windshield wiper motor, spotlight, and outside mirrors so you can see what's coming up behind you, Miss Yoder. Makes driving safer. Spotlight's mighty helpful when you come home from meeting on a Sunday night in the winter. Anyone in the ditch or slid off the road—put the light on them and get the chain out of the tool chest on the running board, and with this car you could have them up on the road again as quick as you can turn a pancake."

Why, it was wonderful—all the ways she could serve others by buying herself a substantial car like this. But where on earth would she park it in East Lynne? Well, first things first. Surely she could get Ike to build her a garage in exchange for some of the farm rent.

Well, Mr. Dorrance and Barbara rode up and down the

east and west avenue of Harrisonville and far out into the countryside, getting the feel of the Buick. Glass in the windows that roll down, wing wells to let the air come in on a body and cool the sweat. The gearshift down on the floor worried her, though, a lot.

"Nothing to it, Miss Yoder, just like a big 'H'. Learn three gears forward and one back—start out in low, push it up to second, shove in the clutch again and move on down here into high." He stepped down on the gas and the motor hummed. Barbara thought to herself, "This is just how a car ought to ride and how a motor ought to sound."

She ended up having to pay $900 for it. The Buick made the tinny Ford look sick, that one he'd wanted $1,100 for. She'd learned from her mother that if you needed something, save until you can pay cash, then don't buy cheap. You don't have to be extravagant, but buy sturdy things and build with quality materials, like they'd done building that big Swiss barn. The barn would stand for 200 years, provided someone took care of it.

Barbara made that salesman get over on the far side of the Buick while she settled herself behind the wheel. She'd take her free driving lesson out here in the countryside. She looked both ways—no one was coming either way. She'd already gotten used to driving her big Chase tractor—this was cream cheese compared to that.

Mr. Dorrance had to have her stop just once. She'd let out the clutch too fast, jerking them both. His hat sailed out the window. It took him only a minute to cross the ditch and retrieve it. This time he wedged it down on his forehead.

Be careful with this old farm woman, don't insult her while she's doing this well. It was really wonderful how she was catching on. He'd known Mennonite women out east of town were go-getters when it came to getting things done. This car hadn't buffaloed Barbara at all.

She did stop the shiny Buick at the edge of town and

let him take over so he could drive it back to the sales room. Now that she had the hang of it, she'd get it home by herself. Only thing she hadn't tried out yet was the horn. But, give her time. Rome wasn't built in a day.

A part of Barbara just couldn't believe it as the other part of her smiled and blessed her calloused palms as they held the mahogany wheel. She'd worked hard every day of her life. She was thrifty and saved her money. She picked gooseberries and nuts, and still sold them. She knew how to cut up the worn clothes for rag rugs, and could keep up with the hired hand come time to put rings in the hogs' noses—why there was no end to the things she knew how to do.

My, how the Buick held the road. That gearshift hadn't buffaloed her much at all, and the clutch let out as friendly and easy as if she were letting up on her sewing machine pedal.

Bishop Hartzler heard the roar of a motor car, a real car. He glanced down the sloping road into the shade of the evening. The gleaming nickel headlights caught the sunlight and split it like diamonds over the glossy hood of the mighty car. He rested his pitchfork in the soft dirt as he stared at some old black-bonneted woman high in the driver's seat of that magnificent Buick.

She couldn't drive past the bishop standing out there in the middle of his barnyard without nodding or waving. So Barbara, mouth wreathed in that smile she'd had all afternoon, dipped her head and let her left hand rise from the wheel, giving the bishop a kindly howdy-do as she sped past. That other part of her that nudged her now and then reminded her that tomorrow she'd have to take time to sort it out and put it together, getting it all to fit just right. Anyway, she finally had her car.

She turned a corner and headed her magnificent car up her street. Her color reddened some as she blushed at such newness. She couldn't deny that her car with the headlights at one end and the covered rear tire adding dignity at the back would attract attention. As she brought the Buick to a halt in front of her elm tree, Arthur Hostetler looked over and saw Barbara Yoder climb down out of a car that would make the devil drool.

Chapter 13

If anyone at the meetinghouse criticized Barbara for buying the Buick, she never got wind of it. Crowds parted in respect as Sister Barbara Yoder drove onto the meetinghouse grounds. The green grass created a soft backdrop for her automobile that purred with perfection. Look how the back seat was filled—and another sister in front with Barbara.

Barbara drove up to the little cement block by the sidewalk that led to the steps, shoved her gearshift into neutral and kept her foot on the brake as they got out. There were six of them, widows and unmarried sisters of the church who lived in her village.

Their bodies swayed in the evening twilight—shawls, capes, and black bonnets identified that they were sisters of like faith. Their steps fell softly on the worn stones and green grass. Like cloistered nuns entering the chapel for vespers, their faces reflected the joy and praise in their hearts.

Barbara swung her car around as the young brethren nodded respectfully. She steered her Buick into her stall in the horse and buggy barn. Barbara didn't like it much—that gleaming trunk with the tailored canvas-covered spare tire sticking out beyond all the rest of the cars. She dropped her keys into her purse and strode with quick and firm steps to the meetinghouse in her attempt to catch up with the others.

Barbara failed to notice the bishop turning toward her with a drawn, sober face. It bothered him that Barbara's automobile stuck way out beyond the others like that. And those nickel-plated headlights rising up like two moons over Jordan. Could it be that Barbara had overstepped the proper bounds of *gelassenheit?* Where was her meekness, her submission?

He decided that he'd better call a meeting of the ordained brethren after the service. Seemed like he remembered hearing that the former Bishop Hartzler once had to have a set-to with Barbara's pioneer mother, Sarah. Gutsy old woman too, from the stories folks still told about her.

Barbara stepped along. "Evening, Brother Diener. Evening, Brother Hostetler."

The brethren nodded and murmured "Good evening" respectfully to her. Who could find fault? Why, even Arthur Hostetler, two Sundays ago, had trouble heading up that hill in his Plymouth after services. The drenching rain during morning worship had left the road a slough of deep, black mud. His car hadn't been up to climbing the clay hill that led up toward Miller's. When he looked behind him he saw that Andrew Kauffman was having trouble with his Chevrolet. Arthur knew he would bog down to the axle in the mud unless he gained momentum. But the hill was treacherous and the road was high in the middle and sloping on the sides. Water filled the ditches on either side.

"Careful Arthur!" Sister Hostetler warned him. He gunned it, but the rear of his car swung around as it came to the hill. Before they knew it, their blue Plymouth sagged, its rear end in the deep ditch and the front end facing downhill. The yellow clay grinned up at them.

"Oh, Arthur, now what'll we do?" cried Sister Hostetler. Two little girls, wide-eyed, clutched the back of the front seat with nervous fingers. Yes, just what would Papa do now?

Then Andrew Kauffman advanced along the muddy road in his Chevrolet. He had sense enough to know that he'd have to surge forward and try to make it completely to the top, then stop and see what could be done for Brother Arthur. Sweating and twisting with his muscled arms and hands, he gunned his car and tried to ease it around the front end of Arthur's ditched Plymouth. His spinning back wheels started sliding on the clay. Before you could say Johnny Cake, his car lay sideways, deep in the other ditch.

Two Model T Fords did pass by, overheated, sliding around on the slick clay. The drivers couldn't stop. They would have to go on up the hill to Miller's and get a team and come back for the Good Samaritan work. Steam rose from their radiators as they ascended the slope.

Then Barbara and her bunch of black-robed sisters came along. The mud didn't disturb Barbara too much. She felt the wheels of her car sink and cooperate with her mighty eight-cylinder engine, humming and purring along in second gear.

Raindrops gleamed from her headlights and outstretched hood ornament. That hood ornament served as a pointer to keep her steady and on track. The weight of the six sisters in the car gave it further ballast. She saw Arthur Hostetler up ahead pulling at a loose fence post, knee deep in mud and water, trying to find something as leverage to pry his wheels out of the ditch. His wife called instructions to him on how to rescue their car. The children in the back seat looked worried—and they were hungry.

"Give me strength," Barbara prayed, her fingers clasping the big wooden wheel. She pushed in her clutch. Steady now. Steady. Shifting down into low gear, she began to turn the Buick out of the tracks left by Arthur's and Andrew's cars. She'd have to make a new track. Driving on the edge. She pressed down on the gas. How silent the car seemed, its sounds muffled by the heavy mud. Had she not been so frightened and nervous, she would have noticed how it felt like riding on velvet.

The Buick made it right up past the two ditched cars. Barbara stopped. She opened her door and looked back to Arthur Hostetler. "Think I can get you out, Arthur." Her Sunday shoes sank in the mud right up to her stockings as she pulled open her tool chest and searched for her chain.

Arthur was simply spellbound at such an offer. But he doubted if even a steam engine could get him out of this ditch. He bobbed and slopped forward toward her, grasping the hook of the chain, hoping his wool pants wouldn't draw up, wet at the bottom like they were. It would take Geneva a whole week to work on his Sunday shoes after they got home.

The big Buick kept humming, undaunted, awaiting Sister Barbara's further commands.

"Your shoes, your shoes. Oh, Barbara," cried the sisters in the back seat. Their bonnets ducked and bobbed as they peered out, just like setting hens fresh thrown into the brooder house duck and bob their heads at the window.

Barbara took little notice of her shoes and stockings. She had made friends with Missouri mud long ago. She paid it a no-never-mind, shifted down into low gear and let out her clutch.

Looking back through her side mirror she saw Arthur's Plymouth budge. She ought to have told him not to spin his tires that way until she had him up on the road again. But anxious Arthur did remember to let up. The Buick hummed and gave two or three dignified movements forward, then stopped. She put it into neutral, shoved in the clutch and tried the low gear again.

"Ain't no use, Sister Barbara," cried Arthur, beat out by having to be towed out of the ditch by this opulent Buick, and by a woman to boot. Slowly Arthur's Plymouth righted itself, and its mud splattered windshield headed her way.

Slowly, the grinding Buick, with its load of six praying sisters for ballast, towed the Plymouth to a safe place at the top of the hill.

Barbara backed down that hill in the ruts her Buick had made. They were good ruts, as straight as one of those furrows she'd plowed behind a horse long ago. She'd just change that Scripture a bit: "She who puts her hands to the wheel and foot to the gas ought not to look back."

When she got to the bottom of the hill she hooked up Andrew's car. With the ruts she'd cut with her heavy car, she put it into low and didn't even have to stop once until the Chevrolet was up there next to the Plymouth. Wonderful how she got the hang of it. The sisters in the back still ducked and bobbed their heads at such miracles. Why, this was better than riding on the merry-go-round.

They all gathered at the top of the clay hill by Miller's huge white frame house.

There was a kind of party laughter; the strain of it all had made them forget for a moment that it was the Sabbath. God would forgive. Then Barbara's quick eye caught a glimpse of the bishop's black Ford approaching that clay slope. She heard him try to accelerate and keep the light Ford in those ruts she'd opened up for everyone. But the bishop's Ford gained too much speed and, wouldn't you know, it bounced right out of those ruts and right onto that treacherous clay slope.

Barbara and her little crowd stared in disbelief as the bishop's touring car, out of control, swung around halfway, then completely around the other way, and landed in the water-filled ditch, facing downhill.

"Well, there's not just one ox in the ditch today, it's a whole herd," said Barbara, climbing back into her Buick, chunks of mud gooing up her floor. "You sisters want to get out this time?" Barbara queried, unsure if they would feel safe for such a three-quarter mile backwards ride down that clay slope.

"Oh, no," they chanted together, "we'll sit, Sister Barbara, we'll sit."

Barbara hadn't had time to think that they might be having fun. By now backing up in the mud was nothing at all. She'd made her track. All she had to do was stay in it. Barbara would have rolled down the glass and crooked her elbow out, driving with one hand like the farmers did, but it was raining too much.

She backed up three quarters of a mile to hook up the bishop's Ford with her sturdy chain and big hook. This time her Buick never paused once. She was getting to be an authority on this. She'd have to give her niece Twili lessons on how to drive in the mud like this.

The bishop had never mentioned opulent cars in his sermon, that is, not yet. He knew why folks at the meetinghouse nodded with respect at Barbara Yoder and her long, heavy Buick.

Chapter 14

One spring day Barbara drove out to her old farm to visit Ike and Mary Barb, her grand-niece Nancy Barb, and sunny-dispositioned little Dave.

She decided to take the children fishing. So they packed a big picnic lunch in an old egg basket, rigged up some fishing poles, tied them on the running board of her car, and off they rumbled through the pasture. She drove down into the little hollow with the flat rocks and shale, then up higher into the woods and the bluegrass pasture. She was a little anxious about easing the Buick down the hill and across the little creek this time of the year. As she descended beyond the pawpaw patch, she saw the water was low and that gravel was showing in the little creek where the verbena spread itself so bountifully.

The children laughed and clutched at her dashboard in glee as the car rocked and hummed, splashing through the clear water and gravel and on to the broad meadow on the banks of Camp Branch, the creek lined with giant oak, hickory, sycamore, and ash trees.

What a wonderful day! The sun stayed mellow, giving off a golden light. It didn't get too hot. The May apple trees still stood straight, waxy, heady with aroma. The last of the Sweet William tossed in the wind. Cows lifted their red and white heads, chewed their cuds, and lowed. White clouds billowed overhead. Barbara taught the children to listen to the wind sighing through the trees, and to know the difference between the sound of the wind and the broadly branched hardwoods.

Barbara, wearing her old blue sunbonnet she'd kept all these years, felt like a girl again as her calico dress whipped about her lean form. Nobody could ever call her a "big Dutch cow." She had eaten heartily all her life, yet she remained agile and lean. Heredity and hard work, that's what did it. Especially the hard work.

They decided to eat their picnic lunch before they fished. An outing always made a body hungry, and the children were fit to be tied. "Oh, Auntie Barb, may I say the prayer for our food at our picnic, may I?" asked Nancy Barb.

Barbara had noticed when little Nancy Barb came over and sat by her at meeting, that the child fixed her eye upon the bishop or the minister of the morning. The child lifted up her clear voice to join with the adults in singing, "The Lord Is in His Holy Temple." She even rebuked her little brother Dave kindly, with her finger over his lips if he uttered a sound. This child was caught up in worship and wonder.

They spread the red and white checkered tablecloth under a shagbark hickory. Barbara set out the deviled eggs and thick smoked ham sandwiches, made with her fresh bread baked just yesterday. She had brought a little dish of graham cracker pudding for their dessert.

How good it felt, how heavenly and earthly all bound together, and to be a part of it all: the sighing of the wind, the laughter of the children, the prayers, the smell of the sweet ground rising up out of the bluegrass. Nancy Barb's prayer would have made a grown Sunday school teacher ashamed—the fullness of it, the fervor and love as little Nancy Barb bowed her flaxen head, folded her hands and prayed, thanking God for the day, for her Aunt Barbara, for her father and mother and for her dear brother, Dave, and for the love of the Lord Jesus in all their hearts.

Barbara made a mental note to talk to Mary Barb and Ike about this child. Nancy Barb was no ordinary little girl. She reminded Barbara of how her mother used to talk about her own little sister, Nancy, buried beneath those ancient pines over by Harrisonville.

She knew the children would plead for her to tell that story before the day was done, and about the old angel of a black slave woman who sang songs that made chills go up and down on your back. Well, if the children didn't get too tired and sleepy, she'd go over it all. Family ties were important; telling your story was important. One of the ways God kept his very own message for his people down on earth going was having them tell their story.

Barbara smiled. The children laughed. They ate heartily, then packed up their picnic things and grabbed their fishing poles and headed for the slope by the giant sycamore. They would try to pull out a few fish. Nothing excited children so much as catching fish.

They caught six fish, three each—flatheads and sun perch, just enough to keep them interested. She made them wash their hands in the ripples of the creek and run in the trees and meadow for awhile, chasing butterflies, gathering wild flowers. "Watch out for snakes," she cautioned them.

Then she settled herself in the shade of a hickory tree. She had always been partial to hickory trees; they turned so overwhelmingly golden in the fall. There in the sweet air, she took out her letter from Simon. Simon Yoder, Doctor of Divinity, a professor and now a college president.

He bid them all greetings and told them about his wife, Elizabeth, and their three little ones, and how it was in the Indiana winters, there in Goshen. She turned a page and continued reading on the back.

Auntie Barbara, it causes me pain to tell you that I am under pressure here, leading this young college. The conference bishops say they trust us to educate the young people of our dear church. However, they come in and check over us, as if to supervise us. Particularly what we believe. They want to know if we are teaching in any way contrary to the doctrines of the church. Of course we aren't, Aunt Barbara. It is so hard to communicate with them. We try not to lose patience. I only hope they are trying to be as understanding. It is so easy to come in and lay down rules and laws. What they can't see is how destructive to growth of the spirit it is.

There are two camps: those who really do allow for education to the fullest and open themselves to its challenges, and those who do not, who maintain their stand, even if they may be in error. Right now, Auntie Barbara, the faculty and I here wonder if the college will survive.

Her heart ached to read of Simon's pain. He'd sacrificed so much, worked so hard, served that college on a pitiful salary, and now was threatened by the bishops of the church. She guessed that he was right. The more we know, the more opportunity we have to choose between good or evil. The sin is not in the knowing; it is in the way we choose. The choosing always is between that which nurtures our bodies and spirits and that which blights and ruins them. The same old question had been faced by the children of Israel: "Choose ye this day," Joshua had said.

Barbara bowed her head and began to pray, asking God to give her an understanding heart, a loving heart. She asked for strength for herself, an old woman, to see the challenges of change, wisdom to be able to see that always there would be a fork in the road and always the necessity for choosing, and that she might choose wisely, because of the love and wisdom of Christ.

Either one believed it was revealed—this wisdom—or else one was given over to the uncountable possibilities for error. She remembered to pray for herself. For her appointment with the dentist next week over in Garden City, and that when he jerked out her few remaining upper teeth, that she'd keep her legs down and not let loose and kick him in the stomach. She prayed for grace, too, to try those new store-bought uppers.

She agreed with Simon. One way was not necessarily right and the other absolutely wrong. Jesus demonstrated that. With a purpose in mind, Jesus broke codes and rules of a religious order, trying to help the temple authorities to see the truth. Do we worship the Bible and "the Scripture says," or the ONE and his ways to which the Scripture points? Jesus clarified that to the scribes and Pharisees long ago.

Barbara looked at her watch. Time to rev up the car and get these children back up to the old homestead. She looked forward to seeing it in the afternoon light as they came up from the slope of the woods. She would never tire of feasting her eyes on that place. Barbara sallied over to the creek and lifted out the fish they'd caught, all strung up on a long buckbrush runner. She called to the children, "We've got to go, dearies, party's over."

The huge car leaned and groaned under her command. She steered carefully to avoid the blackberry brambles across from the pawpaw patch. Good thing this timber trail was dry. If it was wet like that clay hill coming up from church, the tail end of the Buick might start to slide. The car, with its cargo of sleepy, nodding children, rocked gently as it ascended the incline where the tall spread of white delphiniums nodded at the fender of the Buick.

They had fresh fish for supper, among the other things from Mary Barb's garden. Soon Barbara decided to leave. The children were tired; Ike would soon have to carry them to bed. Mary Barb needed her rest, too. Barbara remembered how it was when she lived here. She had often gotten up at four thirty and begun working in the garden. She hated to see young Ike so fatigued, so worn looking. Maybe these young farmers bit off too much, turning tractor lights on and plowing into the night.

The old place tugged at her heart. The familiar sounds blessed her ears—the frogs in the pond, cackle of the hens finding their places on the chicken roost, cows mooing, the bleat of a lamb. Even the west wind at the eaves of the house and in the chimneys balanced the whispering of the two giant cedars.

Mary Barb walked with her out on the wide porch planks. A chorus of tree frogs rose into the air. The first of the evening fireflies lit up the darkening sky. "Mary Barb," said old Aunt Barbara, "Nancy Barb is something else. I don't recollect ever meeting a child so sensitive about spiritual matters, prayer, the church, Jesus."

"Oh, yes, Ike and I have talked about it. Do you know what that child said to me when we got home from the meetinghouse last Sunday? 'Oh, Mother,' she said, eyes all lighted up, 'When I grow up I'm going to be a preacher.' Now, just how do you suppose her father and I will handle that?"

Barbara wasn't all that surprised. She remembered that Quakers had women clergy way back in the Civil War times. It took no special brains to notice that right here in their own church a number of women were educated more highly than the men. They taught Sunday school classes with interest and diligence—of course, the women's classes—but nevertheless they taught. At the evening services, Louise Kenagy and Esther Gingerich gave such good talks on Christian growth that even old Enos Klophenstein, who always slept through everything, stirred and listened, even nodded his head a couple of times. Jesus said that a little child would lead them. She'd have to ponder that one like Mary pondered the things the little boy Jesus did, long ago.

After taking another deep drink from the well that used to be hers, Barbara started her car, switched on the lights, and headed for her village.

On the way down the lane she couldn't help noticing how the west forty, new green corn in it recently cultivated, had eroded. In her time, she and Abram Zook, and Simon too, they all tried to honor the contour of the land, kiss it with the plow and follow it along the ridges and little valleys and creeks. That seemed to stop the erosion.

When the light was better, she'd drive out again and take a better look. She'd see what more she could do for Mary Barb and Ike. And she had decided that tomorrow she must start packing and searching for the road maps.

She'd call Twili soon as she got home. They'd plan it together, their trip to Idaho. After all, she couldn't let a car like this go to waste. She could hardly wait to try it on one of those Rocky Mountains, though, being a prairie girl herself, she'd never seen a real mountain.

Chapter 15

Twili and Barbara felt as if they were flying. They were whizzing across the new Lincoln Highway towards Colorado. One look at Barbara showed what those new false teeth did for her looks. Her lips, red with excitement, parted across pearly teeth, contrasting the gleam of her smile with the tan of her skin.

Think of it—the ecstatic thrill of a trip, a journey of such unmatched proportions in her community. What were the folks saying about her? Whatever it was, let it be lost in the wind.

Of course their journey didn't match that of young Charles Lindbergh, who had flown—believe it or not—nonstop across the Atlantic Ocean in the fog and dark. All alone. He landed in Le Bourget Field in France, though neither Barbara or Twili could say the name of that airfield. Why hadn't he made it to Germany instead? Then they'd be able to pronounce all the names.

The great rolling hills of western Kansas opened before the shining car. Twili planned to take her turn driving, they'd agreed on that before they started out. The open wing wells allowed the late spring air to gush in over Twili with the fragrance of the prairie grasses and sweet wild flowers.

The tail ends of Twili's blue scarf caught in the blowing air. Her pink dress, open at the neck, showed off her fine, fair skin. Her crown of golden hair, braided and encircling her head, shone through her scarf. Her bonnet was packed back there somewhere in the back seat. She'd wear it for church on Sunday when they got to Idaho. Her blue eyes glistened like the flying ornament on the Buick's hood.

Flocks of meadowlarks swept up from the tall grasses and swooped across the gravel highway in front of them, circling upward in the endless sky. The clouds reminded them of giant sails of clipper ships, nodding, dipping, sweeping in the blue of the ocean sky.

Three miles back as they'd crossed a winding ravine, an explosion of feathers and shrill cries rose as a small flock of pheasants swept up, startled from their gleaning in the grasses by the "varoom" of the long heavy car. They rose up, all golden, brown, orange, and green, barely missing the hood's gleaming ornament, turned and sailed over the road and soon disappeared, tiny specks drifting to infinity in that boundless landscape and sky.

"It's the bears I want to see. I've already seen enough jack rabbits, coyotes, and pheasants." She and Barbara had traced their journey on the map. They would be passing through the land of the great Yellowstone. There were bears there, grizzly bears; also towering pines, spruce, aspens, and only God knew what else in those magnificent mountains they had been dreaming about for the past month.

"Well, if there are any bears around, Twili, I'm going to leave them to you. I had all the wrestling with animals that I could ever want when I slipped on a corncob while slopping the hogs. Before I knew it a 400-pound sow was on top of me. If it hadn't been for Old Collie, I'd have been one dead Barbara Yoder. You go ahead and play with the bears. I'm going to throw in my line when we come to one of those mountain streams and catch me one of those brook trout."

"What do you think he—Menno Bender—looks like?" asked Twili.

"Menno? Well, Menno's about my age, maybe a year or two older. He had a full head of black hair, kind of wavy. Nice teeth and smile. Not too tall. I doubt if he ever reached six feet in height like your grandfather. Nice man, good build. Wonderful singer." Why was that niece of hers continually bringing up Menno Bender? Twili knows Menno married Berta Roth nigh on to forty years ago.

Barbara changed the subject. She talked about the quilt packed in back that she'd quilted for her cousin Elizabeth Troyer out in Idaho, the wild berry jams and jellies she'd wrapped in newspaper and packed solidly into heavy cardboard boxes with dividers in them.

One thing about a car like this one—with the trunk, the wide back seat, and the floor space in back—they had no complaint about not getting it all in. None at all. Barbara thought the cars she'd seen leaning and teetering with bundles and boxes tied haphazardly on top of them looked positively tacky. Trashy looking, that's what it was. So she had worn her good black leather shoes and one of her better dresses and topped it all off with her bonnet. If she was going on a trip, she thought she'd better look presentable.

By the third day, towering orange and brown mesas and eroded shafts of rocks rose up over the green of the swaying grass, greeting them in their loftiness like the arm of the Statue of Liberty greeted those new immigrants from Italy.

They could see the purple mountains rising up in the west. The air seemed fresher with the scent of melting snow, the cedars, and the towering pines. They had passed Denver now and headed on up toward Cheyenne.

They rode in silence, like an immigrant grandmother and her daughter, eyes wide, mouths open, at the sight of the New York skyline rising before them.

Barbara ran her moist tongue over her smooth new teeth and began to hum "Fairest Lord Jesus." Her heart was so chock-full of love and happiness.

They'd about eaten all the garden things and food brought from home. As much as they hated it, they would have to break down and go into restaurants along the roadside pretty soon. They'd have to be careful eating in there. You never knew just what it was that you popped into your mouth, or how it was cooked. Might even be eating bear or buffalo.

Casper, Wyoming, was coming up. Barbara got a little sleepy in the high altitude, so Twili had been doing most of the driving the last two days.

Barbara complained about a little sore spot on her gum. It wasn't that she didn't like her teeth; it was just that little pressure up there was keeping her mouth a bit sore. When they stopped for the night she'd rinse her mouth out with salt water. Nothing healed like salt water.

If the folks back home could only see them, thought Twili. She shifted down into second after she took the last turn. The gravel road sloped upward, steeply. The powerful cylinders of the car synchronized with the change of gears.

A majestic range of mountains rose up before them. Twili's heart beat faster. She was a little afraid, and if Aunt Barbara insisted, she'd have to stop and let her drive. She knew that she was only a child in her aunt's sight.

Suddenly Twili had trouble steering. The massive car began to sway, wobble, and drag from the rear left. She thought at first it was the sand in the road that caused the steering problem.

Startled, Barbara shot up in her seat, peering ahead with her dark, clear eyes. "What is it, Twili?" The car lurched and leaned, sagging in the rear. "A flat tire. Child, we've got a flat tire."

Twili wrenched the great wooden wheel. They were on a steep slope. Bringing the Buick to a halt, she thrust it into neutral, while the great engine still went varoom, varoom, awaiting further instructions.

"Turn it off, child. We've got to change a tire."

Barbara had a sinking feeling. She looked around. They were alone. God only knew when another poor, lonely soul would wander along on this slope. Mountains surrounded them.

When Barbara looked to her left, she clutched her throat. "Mercy, child. Look at this chasm," she cried as her black eyes stared into a canyon that dropped straight down to perdition. Twili didn't want to look.

"Put on the emergency brake, Twili. Pull it hard. You get out, I'm going to slide out on your side, too." Her dress caught on the marble ball of the steering wheel. Be careful. They'd come too far and invested too much. She was not going to have her touring Buick topple into some Rocky Mountain gulch. Weren't they used to challenges? Changing a tire might help them work up an appetite, especially after those soggy pancakes they'd had to poke down at that cafe way back at seven o'clock this morning. Don't even mention the coffee.

First thing Twili and Barbara did was to race about and grab some big yellow rocks and wedge them under the Buick's tires. Next, they unhinged the massive running board tool chest.

Barbara took out some funny looking iron instruments. If a grizzly bear jumped out of the woods at them, they had weapons now. Twili began to giggle. Aunt Barbara, too.

"How do you work this thing?" Neither knew. Think. What comes first. Then Barbara reasoned. "We got to get the wheel off back there, that one with the tire all flat and crumbling outward. Get the jack. We've got to jack it up, Twili."

They lost about five minutes bumping into each other, sizing up each tool. Twili thought it was worse than learning how to cut up a frying chicken, and she'd put that off until her mother had finally shamed her.

The gravel dug into her knees painfully as Twili crawled under the back bumper to stick the jack under the axle. She still giggled, until she conked her head on the underneath of the bumper.

"Got to put this unfolding thing into that jack." Twili crawled back under the car.

Then they decided that they'd better get the wheel off before they got it up off the ground or they'd never get those bolts loose.

Twili grabbed a wrench that looked like it would fit over the wheel bolts. "Ugh!" She tried again. She slapped her lips together, hunched herself, and heaved. The mighty wheel bolt wouldn't budge.

Then Barbara cried out. "Hold that iron handle, I'm going to conk it with this rock." She'd learned long ago the effectiveness of a large stone as an implement or tool. "Clang. Clonk." The bolt moved.

"Stop. Better get the spare tire out of that casing up on the back. Once we get this Buick jacked up in the air we will never be able to reach it."

Now that they knew they could get the wheel bolts loosened, they concentrated on getting the heavy spare tire out of its case and down on the gravel road. When Barbara hit the latch with her rock, the tire let loose with a mighty jump and sailed drunkenly, rolling away from both of them. There was a cloud of dust and a swishing "whop!" as it hit the trunk of a huge spruce tree rising up from the chasm to the right. They heard a whooshing sound as it sailed down into the awful chasm that loomed at their toes.

They peered over the edge in silence, like two crows, wondering if they should take off and fly. Their brains whirled, trying to connect and find the solution to this new challenge.

Barbara remembered the pull chain with the big hook on it and the day she had rescued the bishop and others from the ditch. She had it with her. See how God provided.

Twili started crawling down into the chasm, looking only at her feet. If she looked farther ahead she might do something crazy and just go ahead and leap off into the unknown. Besides, Matthew Kauffman had already taken her to services twice on a Sunday evening back home, and that was enough to register things as substantial. She'd better get a hold of herself.

Twili's legs trembled. Sweat beaded on her brow. Above her an old pinched face looked down, bobbing and praying. Twili finally decided to turn around and back down to the tire, holding on to the rocks and tree roots. Barbara eased the great chain and the hook down.

"Hold on, child, hold on." Barbara's voice trembled.

Stones clattered out from under Twili's shoes, rippling and falling into the bottomless pit below. Could she go down any farther? She remembered that Joseph in the Bible was thrown into a pit. But she was far, far below the bottom of the dry well Joseph had been thrown into.

She finally found the tire lodged between two rocks. To her dismay she realized that Aunt Barbara's chain would never reach this far.

Holding to a small spruce caught in the chasm wall, she hollered, "Aunt Barbara, do you have a rope? You're going to have to tie a rope onto your big chain, and even then I don't know if it will reach." Her voice sent chills down Barbara's spine as a ghostly echo resounded through the canyon.

Barbara dug around in her tool chest. Sure enough, she had a fifty foot piece of good, strong rope. She thanked her father, Solomon, for teaching her to tie the knots he'd had to use when he was in the Civil War. She yanked hard, tightening her knot on the end of the chain, then hurried over to the edge and gave the whole thing a big heave. The chain rattled, dislodging more stones. Poor Twili. "Hold on, child," she called.

Twili finally got the hook around the heavy tire and called out, "Heave, Aunt Barb, heave!"

Barbara may have been seventy, and she may have been considered kind of skinny by some of the ladies, but she could heave. And heave she did, grunting and straining.

"Hold it there, Aunt Barb, until I crawl back out. Oh, mercy!" Poor Twili's scream rose up as she forgot herself for a moment and looked down.

Finally, working together, they got the tire up to the top. "Always good to learn how to do something new," Barbara announced, encouraged that they'd mastered it all just fine.

Bolting the punctured tire to the tire rack, Barbara got into the driver's seat. She wanted to be in command if they had another flat. They'd have to stop at a gas station at the next town and get it patched. She could do it herself, but wasn't that why they carried a good spare—so they wouldn't have to sit by the side of the road and patch the punctured tube and put it all back together? They would have a little refreshment while they waited for the tire to be repaired. She preferred grape pop. Twili would have one of those frozen icicles, lemon flavored.

"Fill it up," called out Barbara, as they pulled into the gas station next to the cafe where they planned to have lunch. They were a bit travel worn following their escapade, but still undaunted. They watched the tall attendant with grease-soiled hands, take the crank and pump red gas up fifteen notches in the glass cylinder. Barbara knew that much—fifteen notches up, then fifteen notches down. One gallon. They watched as six gallons flowed through the glass pump and into the tank of the Buick.

Twili and Barbara sat on the wicker settee of the combined cafe and store. Barbara tipped back her head, savoring her grape pop. Twili demurely licked her lemon icicle.

The service station attendant lifted the repaired tire onto the rack on the back of the trunk, latched it tightly, then placed the tailored cover over the wheel.

"Let's see. That's a dollar for the repair of the tire, and six gallons of gas at nine cents a gallon—that'll be a dollar fifty-four cents."

Barbara dug out her coin purse and fished out enough change. "Thank you sir, I surely do appreciate it. My niece and I had quite a challenge back there."

"You are brave women. You've come fifteen hundred miles or more. Of course, not many women—or men either—drive through here with a fine car like that Buick." His eyes wandered over the car. "By the way. I can see by your dress, bonnet, and all that you belong to one of the plain churches. Couldn't be a Dunker, could you?"

Barbara put down her empty grape pop bottle and wiped her stained lips with her handkerchief. "Why no, sir. We're not Dunkers. Twili and I are Mennonites from Missouri. Our people came from Ohio to settle the plains there. We do have some Dunker neighbors, though, back home."

The attendant looked at them both, taking his cloth and rubbing at a spot on the Buick's windshield. "I used to belong to the Dunkers," he said, with a lonely, wistful look in his eye. "Back in Illinois a long time ago. I guess you might say that I've fallen away. Oh, I still believe in God and in Jesus. But you know—the life, the order, the strictness of it, the family. Sometimes I get lonely for a Dunker service. I'd like to hear them sing again."

Barbara held out her long work-worn fingers to shake his hand. "I'm glad you told us that. I can tell that you miss your church. Don't know what I would do without a church or without people of like faith. It would be lonely without a church." She guessed this man was expressing some of what her nephew Simon had written about, the terrible loneliness and the great feeling of emptiness he'd had when he was unable to worship and sing with his people.

"My name is Barbara Yoder and this is my niece, Twili." She shook his hand with a firm grip. None of those dead-fish handshakes for Barbara.

"Benjamin Stoker's my name. Pleased to meet you ladies. Made me feel a little bit like I was home, just meeting you ladies for a little chat. I got the nail out of your tire and patched the tube. Everything's fine. Took time to check your oil and radiator. This is a mighty fine car. Enjoy your trip on west."

They drove on for about two more hours. They had ascended magnificent slopes and mountain peaks. Wild columbine and mountain laurel were everywhere. A white snowfield glittered in the sunlight to the left, melting and trickling down into a small mountain stream.

Chapter 16

"Let's stop, Twili. It's time for a rest. I want to stick my tired feet into that wonderful clear water." Barbara pointed to the left, where the mountain stream widened and flowed through a spread of rocks and boulders before it roared on, splashing and singing past a stand of aspens.

"Don't mind if we do, Aunt Barbara. There's a spot ahead wide enough for the car," pointed Twili, anxious to get down to the stream herself. She thought she might fish up some glistening red and white stones.

They stumbled through the undergrowth toward the stream like cows hurrying through a weed patch to get to the alfalfa.

As they reached the stream, happiness took over. Barbara hung her black stockings on a nodding willow branch. Twili tossed hers on a flat rock, then sat down and doused her feet in the gushing water.

"Oh, mercy," she shivered as she jerked her fine-boned white feet straight up, clasping her knees. "Cold. That's icy cold water, Aunt Barbara!" Then she howled with laughter.

Well, Barbara wasn't going to travel from the mud flats of Missouri to the Rocky Mountains—over fifteen hundred miles already—and show herself too puny to stick her feet into a mountain stream. She plunged her old feet right on in. She laughed. She hollered. She fell back on a flat rock and kicked at the water. "Oh, mercy. Oh my." Barbara was as happy as when she was a child and rolled down the new haystack. "Isn't this fun?"

The water soon numbed their feet so that they didn't even feel it. A brook trout arched out of the water at a fly. The columbine, purple and white, nodded its approval. All was right with the wonderful, sparkling world.

When she'd calmed down a bit more, Barbara reached in and lifted the false uppers that were causing such a pain on the left side. "Pardon me, Twili, but I have to give my mouth a rest a bit. These teeth are rubbing a raw spot somewhere up there." Out the plate came, grinning in her hand. Her upper lip fell in like a collapsed tent.

"Oh, Twili, is mush better," she breathed, her words slurred, diction distorted by the cavern in her mouth.

Twili, the dutiful niece, didn't laugh at her Aunt Barbara. She only smiled and prayed that Aunt Barbara didn't get too sore a gum from her fine new plate and have it spoil their marvelous journey.

"Don't worry, Auntie Barb. I'm sure your mouth will feel better soon. You aren't quite used to them yet. You look so nice with your new teeth. I love you, Auntie Barb." Twili leaned over and kissed her dear old aunt on the cheek.

Barbara laid her teeth down on the flat rock beneath her stockings, then she reached out to pluck one of those fabulous columbines. She had columbines once in her flower bed. You had to watch them in Missouri, in case the sun got too hot. She smelled the fragile flower.

"Oh, look at the blue lupines," Twili exclaimed.

Barbara drew her feet out of the rushing water, tiptoeing gingerly over the gravel to the small spread of mountain lupines. "Aren't 'ese just wunnerful?" Too bad she blew air and her lip flew out without the bracing of her teeth. Oh well, it was a small matter. She couldn't raise lupines in Missouri, not like these at least. "Why, I could ssstay rich 'ere forever." Moisture splattered and the small outburst of air blew out her upper lip again, then it sank back in, drawing itself up on its own.

She knew she couldn't really stay there forever. Life just isn't like that. The majesty of nature—the mountainside, the stream, the trout, the columbine and lupines, the whispering aspens beneath the towering pines—it was a gift. No one can tarry too long in one spot, especially on a journey. Soon they would have to say good-bye and climb into the Buick. They planned to reach Idaho tomorrow. By evening tomorrow she hoped to arrive at her cousin Elizabeth's.

They let their feet and legs dry in the cool wind, then drew their stockings back on, brushed the gravel from the bottoms of their feet, and sank them back into their shoes.

She could tell that darkness would come quickly in the mountains and that soon they would need to find a motel for the night. The mighty car purred on. In an hour they pulled into a little village, parking in front of a combination store-hotel. They checked it out, to see if was clean and comfortable.

"Thissh 'gonna be aw righ,' Twiiia?" Too bad she had such trouble with those s's and those l's.

It struck them both at the same time. Just like the time the stove pipe fell in the general store back home and knocked old Silas Woser daffy. Her teeth. Her wonderful, pearly white upper teeth she'd spent fifty dollars for. "Oh merciful Lord above," Barbara hollered. "I'ff gone off and leff m' teef 'ere by 'e riber, leff m' teef!"

Twili, stricken with pity for Aunt Barbara, held her laughter. She wanted to break out into hysterics. This was funny—and it was pitiful. Poor Auntie Barb. Twili, caught up in fun and glee, felt bad that she had failed to caution Aunt Barbara to remember her teeth.

Barbara made a big U-turn in the village street and gunned the mighty engine back up the slope. The gravel flew. Dogs barked. The mistress of the hotel came running out, disappointed that she might have lost a customer for the night. She could have charged a dollar more for people riding in a long black car like that one. She watched it disappear back up the mountain road. Wonder what frightened them? she thought to herself.

When they got back to the turnout by the stream, Barbara swung her car around as far as she could. Twili got out to give her directions. "No, back up a little more. That's right Aunt Barbara. Now turn your wheels again, you've almost made it."

Barbara leaped from her Buick. She ran through the brush, over a small ditch about as fast as that time when she was a girl and brother Noah chased her with a big dead black snake.

There on the rock where she'd sat, where she'd placed her uppers while her feet cooled and her gums rested, stood a tall man swinging a trout rod, casting flies.

Now what? Twili broke through the undergrowth and stood by her Aunt Barbara.

"Ahem, 'cussse me, misser," Barbara splattered and blew, upper lip exploding with the force of it all.

How could she say it? How would you say it? He might think she was ready for the loony house if she yelled out, "Seen any spare teeth lying around?"

The startled fisherman turned around, consternation in his face at being disturbed in his trout fishing.

"What'd you say, ma'am?"

"Paron me, I don' wanna' 'sturb you, misser, but 'aff you seen any falssse (she slurred the s's again) teef?" Her face turned red with embarrassment. "I mussa lef' m' falsssse teef 'er on a rock."

It sounded ridiculously funny. They all started to

laugh. The man put down his rod and brushed across the rocks. They dug into the nooks and crannies. Twili leaned over the stream to see if she could see the teeth grinning up out of the water. Nothing. Absolutely nothing.

"I've been here about a half hour, lady, and to my recollection, there weren't any false teeth on the rock when I cast out into the stream." You could see him tighten his jaw in order to keep from laughing.

To say that Barbara's heart sank would be an understatement. But they had to go on. Needing time to reflect on it, Barbara let Twili drive. She slid down in the great leather seat, her nose in line with the dash. Good thing the bishop wasn't here, or Phoebe Bontrager either, for that matter. Why old Phoebe would make the telephone line sing and fry, spreading the story in the community. Yes, there'd be some who were jealous of her on this trip and in this car, who'd say it served her right. Barbara began to pity herself. She locked her arms around her waist to comfort herself. Her upper lip, all drawn in, puckered like one of those tobacco sacks when you pull the string.

Twili had the headlights on by the time they got back to the village hotel. By this time, Barbara had gotten hold of herself and drew herself up so that she could look out of the windshield. Maybe it did serve her right, having to go on to Idaho without her new teeth. Pride goes before a fall, her mother used to say. She hadn't rightly thought about it, but maybe she had been a wee bit proud. Things were working out too well.

Chapter 17

If the apostle Paul could do all that missionary work for the Lord with a thorn in his side, Barbara guessed that she could pull herself together and face up to her old boyfriend, Menno Bender—even if it had to be done with her upper lip all puckered in. Maybe he'd focus more on her car.

Barbara had driven again the last day of the journey. Driving got her mind off her terrible predicament. Instead she had concentrated on the river bridges, the U-turns, the braking, the accelerating.

They had been at Cousin Elizabeth Troyer's now for three days and the excitement still hadn't worn off. Elizabeth and her husband, Urie, sat on the edges of their chairs, spellbound, rocking in laughter as Cousin Barbara kept them in hysterics with her tales of the trip from Missouri.

Twili, wiping the tears from her laughter, was telling of how they stopped to cool their feet in a Rocky Mountain stream and Barbara's catastrophe.

"And when Auntie Barb asked me, 'Who on earth took my teeth?'"—at this, Twili bent double and clutched her sides—"I said, 'Auntie Barb, you know those grizzly bears we were talking about? Well, I bet an old grizzly bear came down there to that stream after we left to catch himself a fish and spied your teeth. I'll bet he was plumb tired of his own worn-out stubs and broken snags. Saw that gleaming plate of smiling teeth and up and bit right down on it and galloped home to his cave to show mama bear and the cubs his wonderful new teeth.'"

Well, they were all fit to be tied. It sounded just like a circus.

"Big grizzly bear came up to my car right there in Yellowstone Park. He huffed and blew, and stood up and put his paws right up on the side of my Buick. I rolled the window up fast as I could, and when that big bear spread his lips and tongue on my window, grinning in at me, it surely did look like he was wearing my new store teeth."

Poor Aunt Barbara slurred and blew air as she told the story. Now she could laugh about it and not sit and put herself down. What did it matter if she spit a little fine mist when she talked? Her relatives loved her just the same. Besides, other than her mouth, she was a real well-preserved woman. Hadn't taken on all that weight at the hips like Elizabeth and so many others their age seemed to have done. When she buckled her belt you could still tell she had a waist. And she wouldn't say that the wrinkles in her face made her look old. Rather, they were fine lines engraved in tanned skin. Her dark eyes shone brightly.

Cousin Elizabeth was ecstatic with the patchwork quilt Barbara brought her. "See how it makes my bedroom come alive, all the pink, blue, and white?"

Farmer Urie was thankful for the homemade jams and jellies. He'd picked blackberries in Missouri when he was a boy, gooseberries too. Nothing tasted as good as wild berry jelly.

"I've got to tell you this," cried Twili. One could hardly get a word in edgewise. "We had a little tiff, Aunt Barbara and me. Yes, a little bit of a falling out. We were driving up there near Yellowstone Park, thinking we were lost and bewildered by it all. Then I began to smell something. It bothered me greatly. It just kept up. I guessed Aunt Barbara must have had beans back there in her soup for supper. She claimed she had pea soup. But I wasn't believing her at all with the air that was building up in the car.

"Finally, I had to roll my window down in that cold mountain air. Now listen to this. While I was there accusing Auntie of crude manners and fouling up the very air we were breathing, she was sitting there at that wheel getting all tight, leaning forward." Twili broke into hysterics again. Barbara was ready for the stretcher.

Barbara broke in. "I was sitting there thinking, What kind of a niece have I got in this car with such bad manners? The air was getting so bad in the car. I was put out." Her upper lip blew out a little on that "p" sound. "I'm not one to accuse young folks of throwing manners out the window. But I did start going over in my mind what Twili had eaten that day. Did she order bean salad or soup? Finally, I started laughing. So did Twili. For we were sitting there with both windows down, freezing, and still that foul smell kept circulating in our car."

"Well, the puzzle was solved as we rounded the corner in the park and a sign loomed up ahead, 'Sulfur springs for the next five miles.' It was the funniest part of the trip, except Twili thinks what happened to my teeth tops it."

There is nothing like family. The wonderful joy. The love and acceptance. The telling of all the stories. Urie and Elizabeth took the opportunity to share their stories, too. They also took time to read the holy Scriptures and to pray.

Barbara had misgivings about going to services at their meetinghouse come Sunday. What would the folks think of her, an old Missouri farm woman, looking poor and pitiful, mouth all caved in? With a mouth like that, who would be foolish enough to drive in the churchyard in that opulent car?

If they got invited out for Sunday dinner, she'd have to cut her beef roast or pork chop into fine bits. She'd have to pass on these wonderful western apples, or at least peel hers, dice it all up and shave off a bite with the paring knife as she gummed it, chin coming up like that to meet her nose.

She had always been a woman of courage. Her courage hadn't stopped just because they drove through Yellowstone and the land of the grizzlies. So they went to church with the Troyers.

Barbara's old friend, Menno Bender, and his wife, Berta, came up after the service to meet her. "Why, Barbara Yoder." Menno tried to look in her eyes, anywhere besides at her caved in lip.

"Why it's been, let's see, nigh on to forty years since we last met." He reached out his big tanned hand and shook hands with Barbara.

Berta, a portly woman dressed in a plain dress with the regulation cape and covering strings falling down over her shoulders, reached out and embraced Barbara, greeting her with the holy kiss.

Barbara turned red, but tried to look Menno Bender straight in his chiseled, tanned face, which reflected tenderness and character.

"Wh' 'oudy do, Menno. Good to ssee you." She couldn't think of a thing to say next. "You still singing from that *Harmonia Sacra* book?" Now why on earth did that slip out? Menno'd think she was forward, mentioning the book they'd held together at singing classes, his favorite book. Lord help her.

To make matters worse, Menno and Berta invited Barbara, Twili, and the Troyers to their house for Sunday dinner and an afternoon visit. They wanted to catch up on all the news back in the old community.

Menno thought that Barbara had held up pretty well through the years. He remembered her mother, old Sarah. Those Yoders got almost eaten up by the grasshoppers back when he was a boy. When her husband died, Sarah had dug in her claws and made something out of herself and her situation. Menno had read about one of Barbara's nephews, Simon, who graduated from Union Theological Seminary with his Doctor of Divinity degree and was now a college president. Barbara had a good family.

He just couldn't understand why Barbara had let her teeth go like that. It would have to interfere with her singing. She figured she must have saved all her money for that Buick that all the young men of the church had checked out and admired.

She had some spunk for a woman of her age, to start out with her niece on a two thousand mile journey with the roads no better than they were through the mountains. But then, he thought, why put limits on people. Folks were always surprising one another. He preferred things to slow down a bit. He liked the old ways and old patterns, but why put limits on people?

Women in his church came up front on Sunday night at Young People's Meeting and gave right good talks. So far he hadn't heard of any women preachers. He'd read in the church papers about the Russian Mennonite sisters out there in Newton, Kansas, who had set up an order—kind of like a group of Catholic sisters—and opened up a hospital.

He guessed the Lord led the women of the church to their places and stations. But Menno had a place deep inside where there was a bit of a tenderness about some of the changes coming on in the church.

At the end of two weeks, Twili and Barbara hugged and kissed their Idaho relatives and friends, and loaded the Buick with gifts given to them: two bushels of apples, hand-crocheted doilies for Barbara's china cabinet shelves and a long beautiful spread for the back of her couch, nuts and fruits canned there in the west to take back to the Missouri folks. The parting was hard. Tears slid down their cheeks. They had loved and been loved.

Seven days later, the dust-covered Buick crossed the state line from Kansas into Missouri. Fifty more miles and Barbara would be home. The crops looked good. Farmers had their corn laid by. Tractors toiled in the fields. Horses rested in the pastures. Red barns and silos towered up into the cloud-filled sky. They would get home in time for the first of the garden tomatoes and the roasting ears. Barbara resigned herself to cutting her corn off the cob until she got down to Garden City to the dentist. Getting the car unpacked, going to the bank, and getting new teeth were the first things on her list for when she got home. She hoped she didn't have to go to services at Sycamore Grove with her lip all puckered in.

How wonderful home looks to the returning traveler. Barbara decided to wait until the next day to unpack the boxes. She would just hang up her clothes, get into her nightgown, throw up the windows to let the breeze blow through, and then fall into bed. First thing the next morning she'd go on up to the bank and take out some money for her teeth. Then she would drive out to her old place and share all the news with Mary Barb, Ike, and the children.

The next morning Barbara made a pot of fresh coffee and opened up a pint of pears for breakfast. She made a note to get fresh groceries and produce today, and a new chunk of ice for the icebox. She combed her hair and put on one of her starched dresses, the soft violet one with a bit of lace at the cuffs and at the neck. She grabbed her bonnet, her purse, and a fresh handkerchief, and headed out of the house. She walked down the sidewalk and up toward the store and the bank. She decided to go to the bank first.

She clutched at the latch and pulled. Nothing. The door was still locked. Nine o'clock. Why hadn't the bank opened? Barbara put her hands to the side of her face and peered in through the gold lettering on the door. Yes, there sat Mr. Dave Bradshaw, the banker. Why hadn't he opened this door? She rapped on the glass.

As he rose and came toward the door, Barbara could see that Mr. Bradshaw looked weary and sad. He moved as if he carried the weight of the world on his shoulders. What on earth was the matter with him? He unlocked the door and leaned out, not permitting Barbara to enter. He pointed to a sign in the window that Barbara had overlooked.

"Miss Barbara Yoder. There's bad news, I'm afraid." Poor Mr. Bradshaw looked as if he was going to burst into tears. "Miss Barbara, how can I tell you this. The bank is closed. Last week there was a run on the bank after the stock market crash. We're out of business. Bankrupt. The bank is closed."

Barbara staggered to a worn bench at the corner of the bank that faced the grocery store. Two yellow dogs dragged past her, seemingly aware of the dry winds of hard times that were beginning to soar over the land.

"What will I do now? I've rented out my farm. I've lost all my savings—twelve thousand dollars. How am I going to make it the next twenty years?"

She put her chin in her hand and pondered the dandelions in the road ditch. Barbara's upper lip pooched out. The heat of the sun began to beat down on her. Finally, she got up, shook the wrinkles out of her dress, and forced her feet to take steps over the cracks in the sidewalk. She stopped at the grocery store, bought a small sack of coffee beans, and headed for home.

Chapter 18

In the two years since her trip out to Idaho, it seemed to Barbara that all activity on the land and by the people had ground to a halt. Barbara had read the verse from Isaiah only this morning: "And the Lord shall guide thee continually, and satisfy thy soul in drought ... and thou shalt be like a watered garden, and like a spring of water, whose waters fail not." She asked God to give her the faith to believe those words.

Barbara did not focus her thoughts on herself. She remembered the poverty of the past. It seemed like only yesterday that she had been a girl behind the walking plow. Clods. Dust. Dirt. Sweat. Toil. Then the grasshoppers came. She remembered that back then they would go out to the woods and pick gooseberries and market them. But with this awful drought, what berries would grow?

Ike and Mary Barb broke their backs trying to make it on her farm. Ike did get in a crop of spring oats, but he had to sell them at eight cents a bushel. They pondered long and hard as to whether to even bother cutting the wheat. The crop stood there, anemic and thin, light heads blowing on stalks barely nine inches high. They decided to use the pitiful harvest for feed for the cattle and the hogs.

Last week when she drove out to help Mary Barb take up the old dusty rag carpet, hang the strips on the clothesline and beat out the dust, it had been the simple faith of the child, Nancy Barb, that had given her the courage to face such days. "Don't you remember the story of Jacob and Joseph? How God took care of them when the rain stopped? I believe God will take care of us, too. I believe that the rain will come again someday," she had said.

Barbara wanted to cry when she saw the big maples in the yard of her old place drop their leaves the first year of the drought, and die the second year, their bare, whitening arms lifted up to the brassy, hot sky.

They were thankful that they were spared what some of the folks in Oklahoma and Kansas were going through. All you had to do to know what was happening was to turn your head out west beyond the burned up pasture. They could see it in the western sky—that grey, hazy bank of ever-drifting clouds billowing up. Dust. The dirt and soil of the earth, lifted up by the blasting prairie winds, hung in the air, making the sun look like the red yoke of a spoiled egg.

Most folks took advantage of the winter moisture left in the ground. That, together with the few spring showers that did come, meant they could at least have an early garden. The green beans didn't amount to much. After one picking, the blast of the southwest wind curled their leaves, crinkling them all up like locust skins at the bottom of that dead elm tree. Potatoes? Well, that was nip and tuck. A few marbles dug out of the hard ground in the late summer. That was it.

Folks pretty much limited themselves to a navy bean diet. Sometimes they threw in a ham bone. As long as you could scrape together some grain to feed the hogs, you could butcher. Ike let some of his hogs eat the acorns from the woods east of his barnyard. Eventually, he decided he might just as well butcher them and eat the meat.

Noah shipped seven two-hundred-fifty-pound hogs to market. He nearly fell over when he only got two dollars and forty cents per hundred pounds. Big hogs like that for only six dollars each. It certainly didn't even begin to pay for the feed.

Farmers began shooting their hogs to keep from having to go in the hole to feed them. And money? Who had any? Where would you borrow it? Who could pay interest, anyway?

When Barbara first got over the shock of losing her money in the East Lynne bank, she raked together enough cash to get another upper plate. She didn't plan to eat oatmeal and gum her apples all through the Depression. The dentist only charged her a third as much, and she settled on a cheaper plate. She'd had to sell the walnut dresser taking up space in her spare bedroom. She got three dollars for it. That and the ten dollars she took from the little locked metal box under her bed paid for the teeth.

A new, younger bishop took charge of the church. Bishop Hartzler was worn and tired. He'd earned the reward of not having to be so responsible for everything and everybody, including supervising those smaller churches in northern Missouri and Arkansas, the baptizing, the marriages, and the funerals.

Bishop Byler tended to lean back toward the past, toward a more conservative time. Those flapper dresses—splitting the breeze, flimsy cloth way up above their knees—that the English girls wore jarred him into preaching the sound doctrine of nonconformity to the world.

Barbara believed that a Christian should not be closely conformed to this world. "Be transformed by the renewing of your minds," said the apostle Paul. Just what did that mean? How does one renew the mind? She wished her nephew, Simon, was here to help her think that through. She needed to get a letter off to him. Barbara had heard that he'd applied to teach at Yale Divinity School.

A body doesn't renew her mind by herself. Self-renewal of the mind might mean shoveling in more information and rolling it around in there, might even organize it better into chapters and outlines, but as long as it was only human facts, human thoughts and ideas, the mind wasn't yet renewed. Barbara felt that for certain the renewed mind was a mind that had opened itself to God. Like the lilies in the field opened themselves and waited for God to send sunshine and rain. God sends it, too, provided one turns the face and waits like an open flower.

Jesus knew what he was talking about in that illustration. The mind is renewed when it is opened to God in the blessed Christ. The truth rises up against the wall of all the choices, just like the morning sun comes up against a pink sky. All human knowledge could do was sharpen the mind a bit, provide more edges, maybe more tools, but the real wisdom came from God. Even a child knows that, without even thinking about it.

Barbara finished helping Mary Barb with the carpets. Little Dave and nine-year-old Nancy Barb wanted Aunt Barbara to take them for a walk in the woods and show them all the places where she used to play when she was a girl. That suited Barbara just fine.

They filled up one of Ike's burlap-covered stone jugs with lemonade, cut some slices of Mary Barb's fresh-baked bread, spread them with butter and jelly, grabbed a basket, and headed for the woods.

"Come on, children, see if you can keep up with me." She grabbed one of Ike's worn straw hats on the hook by the door, pulled it down over her brow, and off they went.

"Let's sing, Auntie Barb, let's sing, 'O Sometimes the Shadows Are Deep'." So they skipped through the drying grasses and the hot afternoon wind. The sound of their singing rang over the once verdant land, now scorched and blighted by the sun and hot winds. Only the hardiest ragweed and cockleburs dared show their faces to the sun and wind, and they did so haltingly and with wilted arms.

Their voices rose up from hearts where the water brooks still flowed:

O sometimes the shadows are deep,
And rough seems the path to the goal,
And sorrows, sometimes how they sweep
Like tempests down over the soul!
O then to the Rock let me fly,
To the Rock that is higher than I;
O then to the Rock let me fly,
To the Rock that is higher than I.

They raced down the hill to the first little creek and its gravel and sandbars. No water waited to cool their feet, only blowing sand and hot rocks. A few blackberry briars leaned over, but the berries were only tight little knots of skin-covered seeds. Grasshoppers stretched their wings, hopping and flying in front of their feet.

They climbed through the north woods and up the slope and sat awhile under the two giant cedar trees, listening to the wind in the branches. Great boughs hung down, fanning them, blessing them. Clusters of blueberries cast a rich patina over the dark green.

Next they wandered down to the creek and discovered that it was nearly dry. They could walk across most anywhere. The only water collected in the bend beneath the giant sycamore, and that was brackish, stinking water, filled with little dead creatures. A mud-covered crawdad lifted up a heavy pincer, discouragingly.

Before they turned for home, they stopped in front of the pawpaw thicket and drew back the branches. Even in the drought the leaves had stayed broad and heavy. They crawled right into the very spot where Barbara had crawled the day after her sister, Salome, got married. She had crawled in there and spent almost a whole day in the blessed shadows putting it all together.

That's where they uncorked the corncob from the jug and had cool drinks of lemonade. Then they took their butter and jelly sandwiches out of the basket for the rest of the picnic.

"Isn't this fun, Auntie Barb?" the children chorused together. It was fun. The green cave in the pawpaw thicket provided a refuge from the heat and the dryness. Olive clusters of young pawpaw fruit hung down. In spite of the drought, there were going to be some pawpaws. Barbara decided to come back before the frost and beat the opossums to them. She'd make herself a pawpaw pie.

They sang some more, then folded the napkin over the top of the picnic basket, and made their way back.

When they approached the top of the hill and looked down on her old farm, sadness overcame her. She felt saddened by the weathered look of the buildings on her place. Barbara knew that her nephew and niece were doing about as well as anyone else around here. They hadn't given up yet and moved back east, or to the city. That'd be worse. Who could find a job in the city?

Barbara noticed how rundown things were beginning to look everywhere as they walked along the road to East Lynne. But she understood. Who had money for a new fence? Who could afford paint for a barn? Weathered spots grinned through on some of the houses. Yards turned ugly and dry. Horses and cattle stood, looking desolate, heads dipping toward the stock tank as the afternoon sun blistered the tail of the windmill whirling above in the searing heat.

She stopped in front of the post office and rushed in to pick up her mail. What was this? A letter from Idaho? She'd open it as soon as she got home. First she wanted to wash her brow with a cool cloth, put on a slice of ham with some beans, kick off her shoes, and lift her tired and dusty feet. Then she'd open the letter.

Once she was settled, she began to read.

Dear Barbara. Greetings in the name of Christ. I hope this finds you well. Berta and I often spoke of your visit here. Soon after that, Berta took quite ill. We finally found out that she had cancer. The Lord took Berta nine months ago. She is buried by her sister in the churchyard here in Idaho. I've been thinking I'd like to make a trip to Missouri, back home. I ought to arrive there sometime during the first week of August. I plan to stay with my cousin, Elmer Kenagy, but, of course, would like to visit with you again. Hope to be seeing you soon. Your brother in Christ, Menno Bender.

Oh, the flux and change of time and circumstance.

Chapter 19

The New Deal. That's what they called all these government policies and programs for lifting the people of the depressed nation back up on their feet. President Roosevelt hadn't rescued everybody yet, but Barbara believed that there were fewer wandering people stopping at the villages and farms asking for food.

The people of her community had helped them. They had baked lots of bread, sliced up whatever meat they had, and made sandwiches. Look down the main roads any day and you might even see a family of two or three, pushing a wheelbarrow loaded with their pitiful belongings.

These were hard times. Flatbed trucks rolled by, drearily, backs loaded with gaunt-faced sons and daughters of the Depression.

But then, Barbara mused, hadn't God at least smiled upon her? Like in the Bible, "Who hath believed our report, or to whom hath the arm of the Lord been revealed?" Here she was, a married woman, going on ten years now.

When Menno Bender arrived from Idaho after sending that letter, he took one look at Barbara with her new upper plate and decided that she'd kept herself up right well through the years. She looked a whole lot better than two years ago when she and her niece made that trip out west.

They were married at the new bishop's house. Salome

and her husband, Mose Lehman, stood up with them. Mose still had those pretty eyelashes.

Menno just couldn't get over it. Barbara stood right up when she talked, and looked you in the eye with her dark shining eyes. Her hair had turned a nice, soft white-grey. She wore one of those newer coverings without the strings.

Protecting her brow from the hot sun all those years with her sunbonnet had also protected her face from the ravages of windburn. Oh, she had a few wrinkles, like thin lines in a fine parchment. Her lips parted over perfect upper teeth.

Menno finally got to see what Barbara actually looked like with those teeth pushed back in. It was a terrible thing that happened to her on that trip. He didn't know how she had the courage to continue on with her mouth all fallen in like that. Most people would have hightailed it right back home.

Not everyone approved of an old maid marrying at the age of seventy. Brother Noah had his doubts. "Ought to ponder it and pray long about it, sister. You've made it this far alone, don't you believe that singleness is the will of the Lord for you?"

No, Barbara had never put it in those terms. The will of the Lord was for people to seek the truth, then do it, married or unmarried. She figured that a husband thrown in during her later years was simply a little extra bonus of grace.

Nettie kissed her on the cheek. "Oh, dear Aunt Barb. I know you will be so happy. Menno always liked you. I remember how you used to sing together." Then she kissed her again.

Little grandnephew Dave said, "Well, Aunt Barb must be off her rocker," when he first was told about it. But that blessed Nancy Barb clasped her hands and said, "Doesn't surprise me one bit. Not one bit. Woman as nice as Aunt Barbara ought to have the best of husbands. I do love her so. Oh, and I think Menno Bender is a nice man, that is as long as Menno and Auntie stay in Missouri."

Phoebe Bontrager, when she heard about it, got on her telephone and made the line fry as she rang up her friends: "Why, isn't it scandalous? A woman her age, who kept to herself for all these years. A maiden lady, hooking up with a man? Why, I'm wondering how any man could lie down and sleep with Barbara Yoder. After all, she's done the work of a man all these years. Scandalous."

Barbara's marrying went along with some of the other changes in the church at Sycamore Grove.

Awhile back a group of eight young people from the Bethel Mennonite Church down the road from Sycamore Grove, got up in services on Sunday evening and sang an octet. Four of them had studied vocal music at Hesston College out on the windswept prairies of Kansas. Special music. That was something. It went over more than well. Folks sat there and opened their hearts and ears to the loving grace of the great hymns of the church, of their faith, of the boundless love of Christ.

> Still, still with thee, when purple morning breaketh,
> When the bird waketh, and the shadows flee;
> Fairer than morning, lovelier than daylight
> Dawns the sweet consciousness,
> I am with thee.

Within six months they began to have special music in the services at their own meetinghouse, there among the sycamore trees. Since they had been a singing people—singing always of their pilgrimage, their faith, their persecutions and trials—hearts took to the special singing like May apple leaves take to spring air and sunshine.

It helped them through hard times. Folks didn't dress so well. They drove old, broken-down cars. Most cut down dead trees for fuel for their stoves, come winter. Who had extra money for coal? Only city slickers on regular incomes could afford it.

When the rains returned, you could see the difference in folks' faces: the beaming smiles, the laughter, the refreshment of it all. Children played barefooted in the black mud, laughing as they slipped and fell. The trees lifted up their limbs, leaves opening for the cooling waters. Fish who'd survived flopped themselves up out of the mud flats to rejoice with Mother Nature, whose bounty flowed once again. Frogs chorused in the streams, ponds, and rivers: "Give thanks. Give thanks. Better give thanks."

Barbara Yoder Bender sat in the willow wicker settee on the front porch. The October wind blew through her frosty lace vine, casting a delightful shade. Orange oak leaves hung from a limb over her porch. Menno sat facing Barbara, reading the *Gospel Herald,* the weekly journal of the people of their faith. He kept abreast of the news, and read a sermon or two and an article on Christian growth.

Menno's thick white hair lifted in the breeze, then settled down on his bronzed forehead. He was a fine looking man, even at seventy-five.

"Writer here," said Menno, looking up at Barbara, "believes our country will soon be at war."

They tried to keep up with the many changes in Europe. The news lately hadn't been good. A man named Hitler had appeared on the scene. He spoke with wild and angry howlings, raised his fist in threats, and scowled against the backdrop of thousands of well-armed troops and a fierce red flag with a giant, black spiderlike symbol on it. It made the very blood run cold.

World War II broke out. Soon a darkness like the darkness of the plagues of Egypt, the one where the cloud hid the sun, spread over the whole world, erupting from the hearts of Nazi blackness.

Against the dark skies of the world, giant smokestacks rose up, belching the ashes of the blood and bones of millions of Jewish people, as well as others. It was as if the sun and moon both hid their faces for awhile at the dreadful sounds of places such as Auschwitz and Buchenwald.

The United States was at war again, and again young men of the church had to decide. This time it was not as hard as it had been for Solomon Yoder back in the Civil War or for Seth in World War I. Christians had intervened. The government allowed those, who for the sake of Christ could not kill, to take up the spade and axe and do forestry work in Civilian Public Service. Others donned white uniforms and helped staff giant mental hospital complexes in states from coast to coast.

Barbara had to drive her old Buick to the county seat and get herself one of those windshield stickers for her car, and a booklet of gas rationing stamps. There were also rationing stamps for staples and select groceries.

Again, at the meetinghouse, hymns of thanksgiving and praise rose up in four-part harmony, for they had learned their notes in singing school and Saturday night singings. Their hearts were filled with prayers and their lips expressed their faith: "O for a faith that will not shrink, tho' pressed by many a foe, that will not tremble on the brink of any earthly woe."

Brother and Sister Bender looked to the light of the grace of Christ to lead them for the decade ahead. Barbara's heart nearly burst with joy, in spite of the earthly pains: war, conscription, illnesses, funerals in the community, and all the bewildering changes in the church.

Chapter 20

The great plane, nine seats across the cabin, soared high above the thin clouds floating over the dry Utah desert. Flight attendants took drink orders from the passengers.

"Cocktail, ma'am?" the carefully groomed steward asked, his uniform spotless, his curly hair—a bit long—swept back, blue eyes twinkling.

"Thank you, but I'll have orange juice, please," replied the middle-aged, pleasantly dressed woman in the window seat.

Pouring the orange juice, the steward handed it across the passenger in the aisle seat to the one next to Nancy Miller-Souder. An older gentleman—white headed, dressed in casual, California-styled clothes—took the cool glass and handed it to Nancy, seat belt unbuckled, long legs crossed in her navy suit. A small imitation pearl strand graced her throat just above the pale pink collar of her blouse.

"Thank you, sir." Her voice resonated, like the voice of someone used to speaking in public, before microphones.

"Business woman, maybe an executive. She certainly looks like it. Tall, thin, good legs. Could do with more makeup though," thought the white-haired gentleman, nodding and smiling. He turned to the steward, "I'll have coffee, no cream, please."

Nancy looked at the wide expanse of the desert below the thin clouds, at the fine etchings of the terrain below. Soon they would be coming to snow-capped mountains. She had always loved the Rocky Mountains. They reminded her of her great-aunt Barbara, who once fired up her great black Buick and took her Aunt Twili on an unforgettable trip over the mountains to Idaho. Special aunt, that Auntie Barb.

She lifted the orange juice to her lips, savoring the fresh sweetness.

"Going far?" The white-headed gentleman with the pinkish sport coat and pale silk shirt turned to her. He was obviously a kind, friendly type. His face was interesting, open. "Maybe he's a university professor," she thought.

"To Kansas City." Nancy smiled, her lips parting over teeth as perfect as her Aunt Barbara's famous uppers.

"Beautiful place, Kansas City. It surprises a person. Those boulevards, Ward Parkway especially. There's a famous art gallery there, one of the best. What's it called?" He drank from his cup and placed it on the tray in front of him.

"The Nelson. William Rockhill Nelson. Yes, it's a beautiful gallery, rather famous."

"I'm a Missourian. Born on my Aunt Barbara's place. Everyone called it the Barbara Yoder place. It's a special place back in the center of the fields, surrounded by great woods, a small river and creeks, berries and hickory nut trees. Marvelous place."

"Sounds special. Most folks think unless you're from the east or west coasts you simply don't exist, don't they? All I know is that I was surprised at all the trees in Kansas City. Were you a farm girl?"

Nancy wasn't one of those who tightened up on a train or plane and sealed her lips when it came to the inquiries and friendly overtures of strangers. If the kind man wanted to talk, she would visit with him.

"Yes. I was born and raised on a farm. That was long

ago. I'm not a farm girl now." She smiled wistfully, as if an important part of her might have slipped up into the air and out the window.

"Some of the best women executives I've met were those who came from rural backgrounds. I've found that out by experience. Those women know how to work. May I introduce myself? Adam Martin's my name." He nodded and smiled pleasantly.

"Pleased to meet you. I'm Nancy Souder, actually Miller-Souder, my maiden name and my husband's name." She uncrossed her legs.

"Yes," he thought, "This woman's a business executive. Leather satchel there on the floor proves it."

"Company executive?" he queried.

"Oh no, sir. I'm a minister. I suppose I should say a clergyperson. I'm on my way back to Missouri for a reunion in my old community where I was born. Back near Harrisonville, Garden City, and East Lynne." She smiled, placing the plastic cup on the folding table in front of her. "People seem surprised when I tell them I'm a clergyperson."

"Clergyman, er, excuse me, clergywoman? You could have fooled me. I'm from St. Louis. I work in advertising. I'm on my way home to St. Louis now. But, a clergywoman? You really fooled me."

Mr. Adam Martin looked again at Nancy, trying not to be rude. She wasn't wearing a collar like those Episcopalian priests do. Still, she could be Episcopalian, or Congregational, probably Unitarian. Religion and church history were matters of interest to him. He subscribed to the *Christian Century* and tried to keep up with the development of Christian thought. He was a Congregationalist himself.

"Unitarian minister?" Mr. Martin rested his coffee on the plastic seat back table.

"No, I'm a Mennonite. Our family has Mennonite roots that go back to Switzerland and the sixteenth century.

"Can't believe it. A Mennonite minister? A woman? All the Mennonites I know about would never let a woman get behind a pulpit. I thought you could always tell a Mennonite woman by her shawl or bonnet, or that white cap they wear. Where's yours?" He didn't realize that he was staring.

"Those are religious and cultural symbols that are very precious to many Mennonites and Amish, particularly the conservative groups. The main branch of our church began to reinterpret those symbols of faith back in the '60s and '70s. Though, I suppose in my old home church, you might see a half-dozen women wearing the covering. Old segregated seating styles were abandoned back in the '60s."

"Never would have taken you for a Mennonite, or for a clergywoman." Mr. Martin finished his coffee, then picked up the *Gentlemen's Quarterly* in the pocket of the seat back, stretched his legs, and began paging through the magazine.

Nancy's mind turned back, back to her struggles to be heard. She saw herself as a little girl of seven, drawing up a chair, holding up her Bible and calling out to her family, "Now, I'm going to preach a sermon." They'd smiled, and played with her. Only her mother, Mary Barb, took it seriously.

As a teenager, she mentioned to her father one day out in the yard by the trumpet vine, "Father, I want to study to become a minister of the gospel." When she read, "How beautiful are the feet of those who preach the gospel of peace," she felt a tug and a pull within her inmost being. When she'd enrolled in high school speech classes, she'd demonstrated her talents for debate and for presenting her thoughts clearly, commandingly. Her audiences listened to her.

"Why, Nancy. I don't know what to do with that," her father had said. "I don't really know. Things are changing here in the church. Methodists have women preachers. Those conservative folks in the church wouldn't have it though, would they? Better talk this over with Grandpa Noah."

So she did. She sat on his front porch in the wicker settee. Noah and Nettie maintained the old ways, the old clothing styles. Their faces, smiling and wrinkled, reflected a heavenly peace. Whatever their struggles had been, it was clear that their way had been the Christian way, and that the peace of Christ ruled their hearts.

Grandfather Noah had put his arm around the seventeen-year-old girl. "Oh, granddaughter. Why would you want to be a minister? You know the ways in our church, the Scriptures that speak of women and the places for them in the church."

They had lived through great change. The old ways were their ways—the quietness, the order, the solemnity of it all, the precious silence of waiting for worship, the holy songs in four-part harmony. But they could not hold on to one form, one way. They would not be among those who discredited change with sour dispositions.

Then old Preacher Noah remembered his pioneer mother Sarah. She had been a precious woman of great faith. Her favorite verse had been about oneness in Christ, with all boundaries dissolved: "There is neither Jew nor Greek, slave nor free, male nor female."

"Dear child." Grandmother Nettie stroked Nancy's brow. "I can see how seriously you take this all. Our son, Simon, felt the call to get an education. You know his story. College president. Divinity degrees. Yale theology professor. Still an ordained Mennonite minister. It must run in the family. When you get to college, child, you must go over this again with those who can listen and help you. We love you so." Her grandmother had given her the most precious gift of all, the kiss of love.

The drought and the hard times had become too much for her parents. Ike and Mary Barb just couldn't make it any longer on Aunt Barbara's farm. So Nancy's parents finally decided to move to that college town, Goshen, Indiana. After all, her Uncle Simon once was president of the college.

Her going into the ministry had been a gradual thing, aided of course by the general consciousness raising all over America. There had been women in theological studies for years in their church. Of course, as the bishops grew older and many died, the conferences restructured and many appointed regional overseers instead of bishops. Much of the bishops' authority waned away.

Hadn't their church been one of the first to oppose war and slavery in the young country? The light of Christ shining through that Bible verse greatgrandmother Sarah used to quote shone brighter than any rule or regulation that tended to suppress women. Back in the 1960s in Indiana one of the first Mennonite women was ordained to the clergy.

Nancy's mother, Mary Barb, finished college, too, and became a junior college professor. But it was Nancy's marriage to Samuel Souder that had given her the most courage and strength.

When Samuel finished medical school and the two children, Rachel and Aaron, were in high school, Samuel encouraged her to finish a degree in theology.

Samuel also felt the tug of that verse, "How shall they hear without a preacher?" and studied along with her. They rejoiced the day they were both ordained soon after beginning their assignment at the Peace Mennonite Church in San Francisco, where Samuel had opened a medical practice among the poor. Nancy knew the joy of the love of God flowing through her, giving her the grace for her ministry.

The hardest part had been the college admissions counselor who peered over her glasses, twisted her chin, and pondered when Nancy made it clear that she wanted to finish the theology degree and prepare for pastoral ministry.

"Why would you want to do that? Missionary, yes. A missionary on the foreign field—nursing, teaching—that I can understand. But you, a woman, wanting to be a pastor in a church?"

The tone of her voice and the tightening of her muscles showed her rejection. When the counselor tried to clinch her argument with, "And who do you think would ordain you?" the grace of Christ gave her the love and courage to respond. Nancy smiled, chose her classes, and replied, "I'm prepared to open myself to the leading of God on that one."

Most of the male faculty had supported her more than some of the women. Those years were past. One thing that Jesus had clarified: Truth cannot be tied up in rules, regulations, or customs, but bursts out fresh and new. You can't put new wine in old wineskins. It was not that Nancy objected to traditions and freely accepted rules of order in and of themselves. They could certainly point to important truths, even point to Christ, but they themselves were not the truth.

The travelers said good-bye when the plane taxied to the gate at the airport in Kansas City. Mr. Adam Martin gave her an encouraging smile. "Bet you'll give them one of the finest sermons they've ever heard."

"Probably not the finest, but I do have something important to say." Nancy gathered her purse and small satchel as the doors of the plane opened and she stepped onto the jet way.

Chapter 21

Uncle Seth and Aunt Sonya leaned toward the waiting room window to catch a glimpse of their favorite niece, Nancy Barb. Seth's white hair peeked out below the edge of his brown hat, his brown suit and attractive tie set off his rugged farmer's face. Aunt Sonya, grey hair highlighted with a rinse, parted and swept back in gentle soft curls, waved a handkerchief.

"Nancy Barb, over here. Nancy Barb!"

"Oh, how wonderful you look," cried Nancy, who'd dropped her bundles to throw her arms around each of them.

She kissed Uncle Seth's weathered face. His dark eyes shone. He still carried around that deep sadness and reserve that he'd brought back with him from Fort Leavenworth prison so long ago.

Nancy was home. Intoxicated with joy, she sat on the edge of the car seat, ignoring the looming skyline of the city. She simply wanted to absorb the warmth and joy of those she loved, and to share her love for them.

When they exited from the heavy traffic of the freeway, turning left to the highway that headed over the green expanse of farmland and rolling hills, Nancy finally settled back on her seat.

"Here's the outline of the homecoming service," Aunt Sonya said as she handed the ivory program back to Nancy.

"You are the featured presenter on Sunday morning. See, you are scheduled for the morning sermon." Aunt Sonya smiled, her dear blue eyes filled with kindness.

"I'm honored. It's a great honor to stand behind the pulpit where my grandfather preached for over forty years. Remember the story of greatgrandmother Sarah and how she confronted the bishop about those German sermons?"

They laughed, they talked. They shared joys and sorrows.

"There have been so many changes," said Uncle Seth. "Sometimes I wonder if I can keep up with all of them. Then I remember that the one thing that never changes and that matters most of all, is the love of Christ for me."

There was silence for awhile as the car swept down into a beautiful little shady glen. The greenness still reflected the light of the dew. Sweet honeysuckle stood beside the road, shaking in the wind. A flock of birds rose over the car, flying across the highway and on until they became moving dots against the brilliance of the blue sky.

In another half hour they approached Kohler Hill, which had cut off Solomon and Sarah Yoder from that little band of Mennonites and Dunkers scattered below, way back when the Civil War broke out.

"I remember riding up this hill when your mother, Mary Barb, and I were children," Seth reminisced. "I once helped grandmother hook up the team to a spring wagon. We packed a basket of food and jugs of water, and took a whole day's trip over there past Harrisonville to the East Cemetery to sit awhile at Nancy's grave. Those pines are still there. We found old Marianne's grave over there, too."

"Oh, if those trees could only talk. What stories they would tell," added Aunt Sonya, looking back.

The old community seemed different now. Nancy's parents had been among those who left, long ago. So many of the old timers were gone, buried in Clearfork Cemetery where the old Amish Mennonite Church, where Dunkers and Mennonites worshiped together, once stood.

How the winds of God had blown over this land, healing the awful wounds of the Civil War and the tragic Border Wars. The road beneath the car, once a dirt trail, had borne the horses of outlaws and desperados: Cole Younger, the Jessie James gang, the terrible Quantrill outlaw band. The Quantrills were the ones who burned Lawrence, Kansas, and brought on that infamous Order Number Eleven that had laid waste to the land they now drove across.

"Is that the Sol Miller place?" asked Nancy, focusing ahead upon the stark, prefabricated house and the dilapidated barn, where once a red, gabled barn and a white two-family house had risen up imposingly among the locust trees.

"Yes, it's the old Miller place. That's where Aunt Barbara drug three cars up out of the ditch on that clay hill leading down to the church. She won herself a soft spot in the bishop's heart that day. I think they had planned to set her back a bit because of her showy Buick. She was a gutsy old woman, that Aunt Barbara. The old Buick's sitting in a garage over in East Lynne. I guess I ought to advertise it in a collector's journal."

Something looked new about the country. It was the hedgerows—most of them were gone. They had been bulldozed out, as had many of the fences along the roads. Where once farm buildings stood, now a brush patch flourished, or a clump of oak trees surrounded a well or cistern and the shaft of a weathered roof of some forgotten building, melting down into the earth.

"There are mostly big farms here now. After the war, or I should say, wars, things changed quickly. Farmers needed more land and more and larger equipment. Little farms were abandoned, sold. Once a family could make a living on eighty acres, a hundred and sixty was a large farm. Now folks farm nine hundred or a thousand or so acres. I guess part of it is that our needs changed, too." Seth thought of the luxuries folks now enjoyed.

It hurt Nancy to drive through the little community—her home, the land of her childhood. She could name only a few of the people of her faith who still lived here.

She longed to see the church. Aunt Sonya had written that it had been lifted and a much larger basement dug under it. They had built a new entrance, and even a steeple on the west side. People said that when they drove across the Clearfork bridge just to the south, they could see the church rising up among the spreading sycamores, like a church in New England.

Nancy would wait to see that tomorrow. Today she wanted to walk through the fields to Aunt Barbara's place where she had been born. She wanted to walk in the woods and see how the gooseberries were growing.

They'd go to the cemetery up there on the hill tomorrow and walk among the graves of her greatgrandparents, Solomon and Sarah Yoder, Aunt Salome and Uncle Mose, and that newer gravestone with the name Barbara Yoder Bender chiseled on it.

Chapter 22

She sat alone by Aunt Barbara's grave, remembering. Her heart gave thanks. "Aunt Barb, how we loved you. How courageous you were. How filled with fun and faith like greatgrandmother Sarah."

Her long white fingers traced over the engraved rose and the ridges of the precious name. The wind blew back her hair and gently tossed the grasses. Sunshine and sweetness filled the air. She listened closely, hearing the sighing of the cedars and the sweet call of the cardinal, "Sweet cheer. Sweet cheer."

The blessed words swept through Nancy's mind and heart: "And I heard a voice from heaven saying unto me, 'Write, Blessed are the dead which die in the Lord from henceforth': 'Yea,' saith the Spirit, 'that they may rest from their labors; and their works do follow them.'"

Those had to be the works of such a loving heart as Aunt Barbara's, and of the rest of this family. They had endured sickness, death, and backbreaking toil. Out of it all had come joy, singing hearts, and souls rejoicing in the very love of Christ.

Aunt Salome and Aunt Barbara must have given away more than one hundred of their patchwork quilts. Nancy couldn't even begin to count the comforters, the jars of canned goods, or the smoked hams and shoulders they had given either.

She lifted her head, watching Uncle Seth and Aunt Sonya lay a small cluster of their everblooming roses at the edge of Grandfather Noah and Grandmother Nettie's gravestone.

Could she and her children live as well as these ancestors in the faith had? They were not highly educated and they had no degrees. But they were instructed inwardly, in the heart. They knew the meaning of faith.

In a way, Nancy wished the congregation's historical committee hadn't called upon her to give the speech at the commemoration at the grave of that little Mennonite girl who died in the Border Wars so long ago, her great-aunt. She was too moved. The tears were too near the surface.

How could she do it? She reached down and ran her fingers through a cluster of purple violets that sparkled with the late morning dew, giving thanks for the flowers that opened themselves to the sun and rain.

She trusted that God would give her the words.

Nancy cried openly when she stood looking at the hole looming beneath her feet at Aunt Barbara's old place. All that was left of the large eleven-room farmhouse was this hole, lined with hand-fitted limestone for the basement wall.

It was the place of her birth. Trumpet vines had softened the contours over on the west edge, their clusters of orange nodding in the breeze. She'd been down in that basement countless times, and she had always been afraid. She had never actually seen a black snake herself, only the nearly six-foot skin of one hanging on the water pipe over her head. That had been enough.

In one corner rose the staircase of hand-hewn walnut steps, the ones great-grandmother had tumbled down. That Amish paper, *The Budget,* had mentioned that over a thousand people were at Sarah Yoder's funeral.

The tangle of grass and weeds nearly bound Nancy's feet. Step carefully. Snakes crawled under those boards covering the cisterns. Aunt Barbara took great pleasure in announcing that one of her specialties was taking the pitchfork and forking out a passel of snakes.

The locust trees still grew. Soon they would be opening their blossoms that hung like white grapes, intoxicating, too sweet. The tall blue irises were gone, overgrown by the wild grasses and weeds. Half the pale yellow ones survived, lifting their faces above the choking grasses. In a few more seasons, they too would fade into the earth.

By the edge of the yard, where it sloped down to what was once the lane, wild roses still grew. The bold, pink bursts of blossoms offered hope in the hot sun. They would continue to endure.

The great Swiss barn still stood, lonely—perhaps not yet used to standing alone without its companion, the house. Weathered and grey, a few shingles were gone where Auntie's magnificent peacocks perched and cried and spread their tails. Nancy wondered what the bishop did with the extravagance and beauty of Aunt Barbara's peacocks.

Preacher Daniel Yoder from the Bethel Mennonite Church had helped raise that barn. He got unfrocked by the church for buying a parlor organ for his daughters after his wife died. Nancy entered the barn and sat by the overhang. She looked out north towards the little creek and the timber beyond.

The old creek had filled with mud. Brush and wild berry bushes were scattered through the once-green little glen. A new channel had been cut to shoot the water quickly on downstream. The way of things nowadays—do it quickly and scientifically. The beautiful meandering of the creek was a thing of the past.

The day drew to a close. After supper with Aunt Sonya and Uncle Seth, cousins, and old neighbors, Nancy withdrew, as ministers often need to do. Others do not quite know the heaviness of the sermon ahead, the needed prayer, the openness to God, the required study and right use of the mind in order that the flock might be fed.

Visitors packed the church. Folding chairs accommodated the crowd, many of whom had traveled long distances to be here. They still held to silence before the service. Nancy liked that. "To thy temple I repair, Lord I love to linger there...." It was a silence appropriate for opening of the soul.

Where once only women sat, now men, women, and children sat, mingling together. It was the same on what once was called the men's side. Maybe a dozen sisters still wore plain hair styles and devotional coverings, others scattered on both sides were dressed in traditional American styles with makeup and jewelry.

Some men wore suits and ties, others were more casual, in western or sport clothes. The platform in front, which once held three rows of small pews facing each other for the elderly brethren and sisters, now held the centered pulpit and to the left, a small piano, sound board open so that Nancy's ears received the full echoes of the hammered strings.

"Too loud," she thought. Should have a small grand for better sound, or maybe a small organ. Organ music would fit this rural sanctuary, would bless the atmosphere.

The singing began. It was not like it had been back on the day of her baptism. It was modest singing, accompanied by the piano. One could not especially distinguish tenor, bass, alto, soprano. Singing schools had long been abandoned. Maybe a third of the people could actually read notes. Perhaps the songs in the *Mennonite Hymnal* were too difficult for the audience, over half of whom came to the church from the community. Someone had done a good work, reaching out.

Nancy didn't think this church, rural and isolated as it was in this beautiful little glen, would go the way of most country churches whose doors had closed and eventually melted down into the earth.

So Nancy stood with the minister, Delbert Yost. Together their voices joined in singing "A charge to keep I have, a God to glorify, a never dying soul to save, and fit it for the sky."

Minister Yost's prayer for the congregation and for the touching of God in the hour was genuine and moving. The reading from Ephesians blessed Nancy's soul and heart: "Blessed be the God and Father of our Lord Jesus Christ, who hath blessed us with all spiritual blessings in heavenly places in Christ."

A blessing. Those words, "He hath chosen us ... he hath made us acceptable in the beloved ... he might gather together in one all things in Christ ...." What could be more appropriate as a background for her sermon?

Nancy rose behind the pulpit where her grandfather had preached for over forty years, and faced the audience where, even at the time of her baptism, plain-clothed men and women had sat on separate sides. So many changes had happened. Yet here they were, waiting before her, waiting, she hoped, for a message of faith and hope.

She spoke of the love of Christ, a love she had experienced and that had blessed her, right here in this community—in her day, in her time, in her family. She told of the faith of the first Mennonite couple, Sarah and Solomon Yoder, who came to this county back in 1860. She spoke of what looked like tragedy and heartbreaking sorrow, but had actually opened folks to sustaining grace when their eyes were focused upon the Christ of the cross.

A Christian cannot avoid the cross. Nancy's voice rose up: "The cross is our true home, the place of the greatest affliction, to feel abandoned even as Jesus felt. And yet, it is the place of greatest love. If you would be Christ's, take up the cross."

Nancy spoke of the way of the cross—of self-denial, of refusing to harm others—that is possible only through the grace God gives. It is not humanly possible to forgive one's enemies, but it is possible in Christ. She risked preaching the historic nonresistance of her faith: "Those who take up the sword, perish with the sword." This lesson was hard to hear and denied by many who called themselves followers of Christ. Nancy's message was a Christ-centered message, given to her by Christ himself.

Many who knew her kissed and hugged her, and her hand felt warm from all the handshakes she received as she stood at the entrance with Reverend Yost following the service. A few did not smile, offering weak handshakes. Gertrude Miller, Bible under her arm, looked at her sternly: "Was that the new Bible you were reading from? And what do you do with Paul's teachings about women in First Corinthians chapter eleven?"

There had not been perfect agreement. Change comes slowly. Since Sister Miller passed on by with her stern look, Nancy didn't have time to respond to her questions.

It had been hard not to overeat at the bountiful spread in the church cottage sheltered under the oaks where the old horse and buggy barn had once stood. Leah Stutzman saved a generous piece of wild gooseberry pie for her. Nancy savored each morsel with its delicate flavor.

Nancy had not expected so many to gather for the afternoon memorial service. It had taken some extra time to even find the old East Cemetery. "Look for the pine trees," they'd been told.

The pine trees still rose up. Beautiful red-brown bark scaled up the tall, sweeping trunks. The blue of the sky cast a perfect backdrop for their graceful tops that whispered in the wind. The whispering of the pines made Nancy feel sad. It was as if they spoke of eternal things, as well as earthly sadness in human hearts.

About a hundred people gathered—relatives of Sarah and Solomon Yoder mostly, some quite distant. A small weathered gravestone leaned to one side. Looking closely, they could read the stained, eroded lettering: "Nancy Yoder, 1851-1863, Asleep in Jesus."

"Let us begin in silence. Let our hearts open to the sounds of this prairie cemetery. Let us hear the murmured blessings and prayers of the pines that were here when this child was laid to rest," Nancy began.

Billowing white clouds drifted gracefully above. Queen Anne's lace fringed the eastern part of the small cemetery, nodding and blessing the earth. Nancy stepped carefully in order not to crush several clumps of celestial lilies that spread around her feet.

"The first people of our faith, Samuel and Sarah Yoder and their little daughter, Nancy, came to this spot in the year 1860. If you look over to the left and southward by that stand of cottonwoods and oaks, you will see the land they selected for their farm."

She read a brief outline of the story of Sarah and Solomon's lives. She told of the fearful tragedies brought on by the Border Wars and of their terrible suffering.

"Great-grandmother Sarah used to tell me the story of her little daughter of the prairies, Nancy. About how she loved to sing the songs of faith and how she read from the *Martyrs Mirror* by candlelight. We were always told that Nancy, buried here, was a child of faith. She looked forward to the end of the war when her people could again assemble for worship, and to her baptism. We must mention the contribution of Marianne, a slave woman, who was befriended by Sarah and Nancy, during the worst of the war years. I can still hear Aunt Barbara hum and sing some of the heartbreaking songs that dear old woman sang over this land, over this grave. 'Oh, Mamma, don't you weep for me,' and 'Watch and pray, watch and pray.'

"It was told in our family that Marianne saved great-grandmother's life with her healing skills, and with her soul-moving prayers the night Aunt Barbara was born over there where those cottonwoods rise up. Let us give thanks for the gifts given to our family by this Christian woman, a slave woman who was free in Christ. She was shot and died in Sarah Yoder's arms over there by the courthouse as they were attempting to obey the Order Number Eleven that brought desolation and destruction to three counties.

"Their lives challenge us. They challenge us to live by the same faith, the faith of our fathers and our mothers. My own mother, Mary Barb Yoder Miller, used to read Nancy's favorite story from *Martyrs Mirror* when we were children. Her mother, Nettie Yoder, had read it to her, and great-grandmother Sarah had read it to Grandfather Noah, Salome, and Aunt Barbara."

Turning to the giant, worn book, Nancy opened it to the pages that told of the two little girls whom the first Nancy Yoder had named Mary and Martha. She read with tears in her eyes, the account of their faith and martyrdom, and how they called out to their tormenters, who had woven crowns of weeds and straw and shoved them on their heads, "Oh, how blessed we are to be so crowned, even as the Lord Jesus wore a crown of thorns." They went to the stake, words and songs of faith lifted up from their hearts.

The wind had ceased for awhile. The three pines, kissing at the top, reminded one of the blessed love shared by the Trinity—the Father, the Son, and the Holy Spirit—in perpetual communion. The tall, rugged trunks, reminded them of the one who was "lifted up," in order that all might come to him.

Nancy challenged them that day to renew the faith of their fathers and mothers, the almost forgotten pioneers in this land. She asked them to remember their tragedies, their sufferings, and most of all, their victories in Christ.

They sang in four-part harmony, "Faith of Our Fathers." They changed the second verse and sang, "Faith of Our Mothers."

Faith—living still—cannot be contained in one land, in one culture, in one language. That transcending faith was so clearly understood by the little daughter of the prairie winds, Nancy Yoder, her mother Sarah, and her father, whose heart was almost torn apart by agonizing choices during the Civil War. And it was understood by the mighty wisdom of the one who knew the meaning of suffering, for it was etched in the scars on her back, and was transmitted into love in her giant hands—Marianne.

When the worshipers parted among the blue and green celestial lilies and the Queen Anne's lace, they left with hearts warmed in the knowledge that nothing really passes away for those who are bound in faith to Christ, in whom there is neither Jew nor Greek, slave nor free, male nor female.

THE END

About the Author

As a child, James D. Yoder longed for a church and he found it among the Swiss Mennonites in Cass County, Missouri. "Mennonite women were my Bible school teachers. I will never forget the faith in their hearts, their singing voices, and the love of Christ reflected from their smiles."

Following an early period as clergy in the Mennonite Church, James continued his studies in counseling psychology. He holds B.A., B.S.Ed., and Th.B. degrees from Goshen (Indiana) College and Seminary, M.A. from Central Missouri State University, and Ph.D. from the University of Missouri, Kansas City. He is a licensed psychologist with fifteen years of university teaching and counseling experience, the last eleven at the University of Missouri, Kansas City. James founded the Kansas City Chapter of the Viktor Frankl Institute of Logotherapy.

Interested in writing at an early age, James's poems were published in the *Cass County Democrat.* His story about his experience with the Mennonites is told in *The Yoder Outsiders* (Faith & Life Press, 1988). His second book about his Missouri roots is *Sarah of the Border Wars* (Faith & Life Press, 1993). He lectures widely on issues of spirituality in mental health and does storytelling from his life and writings. He is now working on his seventh book.

After nearly thirty years in Kansas City, James and his wife, Lonabelle (Jantzi) Yoder, continue their lives in Hesston, Kansas. They have one son, Michael. Their daughter, Angela, died at the age of eight.

BERLIN MENNONITE CHURCH